For Joan -
with best
wishes for your
writing —

Joanna

CHARLIE AND THE CHILDREN

CHARLIE AND THE CHILDREN

a novel by

Joanna C. Scott

Black Heron Press
Post Office Box 95676
Seattle, Washington 98145

Copyright 1997 Joanna C. Scott. All rights reserved.

ISBN 0-930773-46-2

Cover art: Phillip Brazeau

Editorial assistance: Debra Schneck

Published by:
Black Heron Press
Post Office Box 95676
Seattle, Washington 98145

For Vu Hai, whose father called him Freddy

HOW THEY TOOK HIM

When they took him he was flat on his belly on the jungle floor, head turned up to see, arm raised, finger delicately touching the tip of one spike.

He had heard about this booby trap before: the flying mudball, some called it, or the flying mace. But he had never seen one until now. It swung gently back and forth in a slow arc at the end of its vine, head height for an average man, neck for a tall one.

Lou was tall but he must have sensed it coming, started to go down. It had ripped the head right off his body. Whoosh. Decapitated.

And then whack, whack, whack, down the line so fast they didn't have time to drop, taking pieces out of them. Dan lost the top of his skull. Harold T. Booker lost a shoulder and one side of his face. Sal was sliced open six different ways. They were all dead, Mack too, and LT, torn apart, pieces ripped off. A low swishing through the jungle air, hardly heard against the drip drip onto the soft rotting underbelly—drip drip—then whoosh, and that was it. Whoosh. Dead.

Charlie, bringing up the rear a few yards behind, didn't see it happen. The others were just around the curve of the trail and he hadn't quite reached it.

Whoosh. Five hundred pounds of mudball spinning down, silent on its vine, spiked all over with bamboo knives, cutting a swathe of death by mutilation.

He heard the whoosh and a series of thumping whacking sounds, fell flat on his face. There were no screams or shouts, just the whoosh and the thumping and then he fell flat and then nothing. Silence. Just the drip drip of the jungle.

He crawled along the line of bodies sprayed across the track. One at a time, one at a time. Dead, dead, all dead. And the radio gone, smashed apart. Useless. Whoosh.

He reached up his hand and touched one of the spikes. Sharp as a razor. Lou had missed the tripwire. He'd lost his concentration. Whoosh. Dead.

That was when they took him, lying there on the path, reaching up to feel one bloodied spike. Got him there, lying amongst the bodies, in the blood, someone's brains, reaching up to feel what killed them. He didn't hear them coming and at first he could only see one of them. He was small and slight and very, very young; ten maybe, or twelve, fourteen at the outside: a boy.

He said nothing, just flicked the end of his rifle. He was thirty at least: a man.

He flicked the rifle again. "Up," he said.

He was only ten after all; no more than twelve.

Charlie stood, awkwardly levering himself

off the slimy ground, keeping his eyes away from
Lou's face and on the face of the black-clad child in
front of him.

Their eyes met.

Oh God, this child was a thousand years old.
In his eyes were battle scars from wars older than he
would ever be. China had fought for these eyes and
his ancestors had fought to take them back; they had
fought the Chinese for them and then they had fought
each other. France had claimed them in the name of
Christ; and the French army had taken them by force.
Japan had taken them then; and famine had marched
in them. The French had come for them again; and
now America. The battle had gone on and on.

The Chinese, though, were gone, long gone;
and the Japanese gone too. The French as well; and
soon would go America. Jesus Christ had stayed, a
determined invader, but he would go, along with the
Buddha. Famine had stayed, and disease, and death,
sudden and horrible. But all of them would go when
the south was liberated and the foreign oppressor
banished forever and family united with family and
there was peace and prosperity throughout the land.
Charlie stood there frozen, staring as age-old battles,
half-seen and uncomprehended, tore at the air about
him; and the child, the enemy, his namesake, stared
back at him with ancient eyes.

In that moment Charlie knew that the war was
lost; he dropped his gaze and raised his hands over

his head.

He was never sure afterwards how many of them there were, although the ancient child seemed to be in charge. He walked behind, prodding at Charlie's back from time to time with the muzzle of the rifle. Beyond that they didn't touch him: no ropes, no blindfold. But his captivity was complete nonetheless and he went with them almost willingly, turning his back on the war and the death on the trail and the responsibility of staying alive and keeping the others alive.

The one in front had a bicycle, an extraordinary thing. There was nowhere here he could ride it and the trail was steep and narrow, punctuated by fallen limbs and half overgrown by the reaching lushness of the forest floor. It was hardly a trail at all, just an easing in the denseness; which was where Lou had made his first mistake. He'd taken them along a trail, not realizing it was one. They never used trails because the booby traps were on the trails. But Lou had been distracted that day.

And then he'd made his second mistake: he'd missed the tripwire. Whoosh. Dead.

Far in the distance Charlie heard the whipping cry of a bird and all around the soft drip, dripping of the jungle like tears falling onto the padded floor.

The one with the bicycle was a boy too. He

moved with a boy's slick movements, his bones working cleanly in their sockets, his feet reaching for each hold with the deft certainty of youth. But the ground was wet and slippery as glass and the bicycle slipped from time to time and the back wheel skidded, crashing once into Charlie's knees. With his hands clasped over his head his balance was poor and he slipped and fell, sliding backwards down the now almost vertical path.

The ancient child prodded him again. "Up," he said, and waited. Then they went on their crazy way, the bicycle slipping and sliding in front and the rifle jabbing from behind.

There were others, how many he couldn't judge, travelling with them through the jungle, as silent as hunters and as invisible. He knew they were there only by the occasional call one to the other and once a low whistling, and after a while they weren't there any more. He was alone with these two child men, struggling with the undergrowth and once with a sudden awful urge to laugh: he was a soldier, like it or not, a man of combat, a warrior, taken captive by children like a frog or a cricket.

The terrain flattened out and they were on a broad, open plateau with the mountain falling away on one side and jutting sharply upwards on the other. The owner of the bicycle clambered up onto its seat and set his feet on the pedals, riding lead across the bumpy ground. They headed directly for the mountain wall and Charlie was not surprised or puzzled because somehow he had been expecting this. He watched for the tunnel opening and didn't see it until the cyclist rode right into it.

Charlie was riveted. He stared at where the bicycle and its rider had vanished, half expecting them to reappear, like a magician's trick, for the rider to dismount and bow and the audience to break into gasps and cheers and excited clapping.

But there was no audience, only himself and the ancient child and the jungle sighing.

The rifle jabbed sharply at the small of his back.

"In. Go in."

He ducked his head and followed the cyclist into the mountain.

HOW HE SAW THE WORLD FROM
A DIFFERENT ANGLE

His hole was at the end of an access tunnel that turned off suddenly from the main one and dropped low, scraping against his back as he shuffled through it, hauling himself with his elbows, pushing with the toes of his boots. At the end it bulged out: maybe six by six or thereabouts and four high. That was his hole. It was black.

Charlie learned its dimensions by feeling and he found the bars back at the far end of the access tunnel by feeling too, crawling back down there, one careful hand in front of his face, feeling around the walls and the floor until he came up against them. They seemed to be made from the same sort of bamboo they used for punji sticks, the same they used for spiking flying mudballs. They were woven into a wooden grid too small to squeeze through but wide enough for him to thrust his arm through to the shoulder.

Feeling around the edges, Charlie thought at first that the ends of the sticks were embedded in the walls and floor of the tunnel and so he thought that when he got the lay of the land he would start to dig them out, gradually work the earth out from around

them. If they had been buried, they could be unbur-
ied. It stood to reason. He would wait until he got the
lay of the land though. He backed away and settled
himself to wait.

But it was black down there and silent, the
walls of his hole were closing in on him and he knew
he never would get the lay of the land, so he slid
down the tunnel again, not so carefully this time
because he knew the walls were clear of obstacles,
and stuck his arm through the bars, feeling around in
the black out there. It made him shiver. Strange, that.
His own piece of black on this side of the bars seemed
to have a different texture from the black on the other
side. He knew what was on this side pretty much by
this time: nothing. On the other side there could be
anything, anything at all: snakes, rats, poisoned darts.

But surely not rats: by now rats would have
come through the bars into his piece of dark to inves-
tigate him, to see if he was good to eat. And even if
they didn't come through the bars, he would at least
hear them moving around.

No, there was nothing living out there. Booby
traps though; could be.

He felt around carefully, turning his face away
like a blind man, looking with his fingertips. And
there went his plan to dig out. The bars were wedged
in hard by two pieces of bamboo as thick as a man's
arm. They made an angle with the floor of the tunnel
out there somewhere in the dark, jammed up tight

against the bamboo grid, holding it in place.

Charlie couldn't reach to where they made their angle with the floor but he knew it was there because he could reach his arm down towards it in the dark and he could see it in his head: a sharp angle drawn on a schoolboy's work paper.

And this, children, is an angle of forty-five degrees.

The only way to dislodge the grid would be to jerk upwards on the struts at this end, jerk hard and knock them upwards. He stuck his arm through, up to the shoulder, but he couldn't get it into a position that would give him the leverage for a jerk like that. The tunnel was too low. He could feel how it might be done but he couldn't get his arm around to do it.

He ran his hand down the right-hand strut again, then the left. If he could reach the angle with the tunnel floor, he could dig it out at that end. But he couldn't reach. It wasn't far, though, from the end of his fingertips. He could tell that. He turned his head blindly again and looked with his fingers, calculating. Just a few inches. Out there, just a few inches beyond his reach was the angle. If he just had longer arms. Or if he had something to work with, a stick, a spoon, even a pen.

He slid backwards down to his hole and went though his pockets. Nothing. They'd taken everything useful. They'd left the letters, though, the letters from Lou's wife. Damn those letters. It was those letters had got him in here.He propped his back up against the wall and thought about the letters. There were rubber bands around them. One red, one green. He remembered the colors, looking at them in the dark. He could look at them up close or far off. He could move them around in front of his face. One red rubber band, one green.

He looked at them from every angle, thinking about what he might do with them. He couldn't dig with a rubber band. No good for digging. He needed something to dig with. Rubber bands were no good for that.

He went over himself again, feeling carefully. He still had his belt buckle. He measured it with his fingers. No good. Not long enough. He had buttons. No good. Dog tags. No good. What else? Nothing. No knife. No gun, of course. No pen. No spoon. Nothing.

He shuffled his back against the wall, settling an itch like a bear on a tree. It was chiggers; he was already getting infested with them. Wasn't it Winston Churchill who had said that the greatest satisfaction in life is to scratch where it itches? Winston Churchill, a great leader of men. He certainly knew what was important to soldiers: scratch where it itches.

But he was wrong. Don't scratch it. It'll get infected. Ignore it, try to ignore it.

He thought about the angle out there in the outer darkness and after a while he dreamed about it, a forty-five degree angle, very neat and clean on a white page, one arm red, one green.

See, children, a forty-five degree angle.

The angle of the dangle. Try to see the world from my angle. What's your angle?

HOW HE ITCHED AND LOOKED FOR
A VENTILATION SHAFT

Charlie woke with panic rising like vomit at the back
of his throat. They were coming for him.

His bowels turned to water and he clenched
his thighs together to contain it. The itching started
up again in a sudden rippling swoop across his chest
and down along one side of his ribcage. He pulled his
legs up into his belly and hung on tight to his bowels,
peering into the dark.

There was a slithering sound and a grunt and
a watery light appeared at the entrance to his hole,
then a candle with an arm attached. A head appeared
after that: the ancient child.

The cyclist came next, dragging a bundle.
Charlie wondered what he had done with his bicycle.
He had ducked his head and followed it into the
mountain but when he had got there only the rider
remained. The bicycle had vanished, a magic disap-
pearing bicycle.

He had tried to memorize the tunnels they
had brought him through but they had gone up and
down through trapdoors and up and down again,
and he had lost track. He had listened for the war,
waiting for the earth to move and shudder, to hear a

far-off rumble; but he heard only silence and concluded from this that he was deep inside the earth. Yes, he was deep down; he was sure of that. He wondered if the war was up above him now.

He squinted his eyes in the weak glare and said nothing, just held onto his bowels while Man One silently set out the contents of the bundle. There was a lump of something shapeless unrolled from a piece of crumpled paper: food, Charlie presumed, but his stomach didn't respond to the thought. Then there was his canteen. He heard the water slosh inside it and wondered if it would be better to drink it and die of some tropical disease or to go without and die of thirst.

The last thing was a large, squat jar and Charlie stared at it, puzzled, until his twitching bowels told him what it was for. He willed himself not to let go.

He nodded. "Thank you."

He wanted to ask what they were going to do with him but all he could think about was that jar.

They gave him no chance to ask anyway. "Eat," said the ancient child. "Drink." The jar he ignored. Then they left without another word, taking the candle with them, leaving him in a blackness denser, it seemed, than before.

Charlie lunged for the jar, feeling around until his fingers closed over the rim. He maneuvered himself into position awkwardly under the low ceiling of his hole.

His hole stank now but at least he had not had to foul the floor. He propped himself up against the wall and breathed very carefully and after a while he didn't notice it so much. He thought about the shapeless lump of food and his stomach contracted, rejecting the idea; but he reached for it anyway and found a ball of sticky rice, a couple of mouthfuls, gritty and tasteless but it was food so he swallowed it down and tried to ignore the canteen until the thought of water overcame the fear of disease and he drank. Then his bowels began to work again and he struggled himself back into position and hoped it was just fear and not dysentery.

The stink was back now, making his nostrils twitch and turn in on themselves. He still had his flak jacket. He had been using it as a pillow. Now he took it and stuffed it into the top of the jar. But it did no good. He could still smell it.

He leaned back against the wall, as far from it as he could, and waited to get used to the smell.

The chiggers started up again. He rubbed his back carefully on the wall, turned his mind resolutely from the itching and thought instead about getting out of here.

He had to stay fit to start with: he had to exercise.

He couldn't stand upright but he could lie flat out. He did some leg lifts and started situps, ducking his head as he came up, but he got breathless so he stopped. The air was hot and thick and it sat heavily in his lungs. Either he could use up all the oxygen down here trying to stay in condition or he could breathe and get weak and stiff. Either way he lost.

He chose to breathe. It was the only choice when it came right down to it.

He propped himself up against the wall again and thought about the bamboo rods jammed up against his cage door. He watched the angle in the dark. What's your angle? My angle's straight up. Or straight down, depending on which side you're on. Seen from the American side, his angle was straight down. From the enemy's, it was straight up. My angle's straight up, to the air.

The air. There must be a ventilation shaft in here somewhere. He would find it, dig it out, burrow up it, get to the top.

He began to search, crouching his way around his hole, feeling all over the roof with the eyes in his fingertips. Maybe it came in low; he searched the walls, went back over it all. Somewhere he'd missed it. Try again. There it is. No, not it. There. No. What's that? A root. That's where the chiggers bred, he'd heard. Snap it off, crawl down to the bars at the end of his black hole and throw it through as far as he could throw.

Get rid of those chiggers.

But he didn't, of course. They had got into his

armpits and his groin, his hair, behind his ears. He could see them there in the black, under his skin, burrowing, burrowing, living off him. Don't scratch it. Don't get it infected. Better to itch than to die of gangrene here in the dark.

He couldn't find the ventilation shaft. He went over the entire surface again and again, obsessively, measuring off segments in his mind, planning it like a military campaign. Now this sector, now this. We've got it cornered now. Nothing. It wasn't there. There was no ventilation shaft. Yes there was. Just over there. He'd missed it. It was in the little area in the corner that he'd missed. Yes, over there. Crouch, reach up carefully, get it before it vanishes in the earth. It's gone again. But wait. Keep very quiet. Watch. Listen for it. It'll come back. Come back out of the earth. Can't hide in there forever. Got to come up for air.

Nothing. No ventilation shaft. Breathe very carefully. Don't use all the air. Careful now. Shallow breaths. Don't panic. And don't scratch, don't scratch.

HOW MAN ONE ASKED HIS NAME

He waited for them to drag him out of his hole and interrogate him. He'd heard they did bad things, torture.

But nothing.

They just kept him alive and left him there, came from time to time to stare, crouching with their knees splayed out, making his hole crowded with people, talking back and forth to each other, discussing him, nodding their heads side to side and making quick movements with their hands. They acted like children, nervous and fascinated, treated him like a curiosity, an odd creature in a cage, and the thought kept coming back that he was not a prisoner of war at all; he was a child's toy.

If he spoke or moved suddenly, they flinched back and the cyclist jerked his rifle threateningly. He wasn't the leader though. He was the backup kid, the kid who trails along through the playground wailing, "Wait for me. Let me play too."

But being the follower did not make him any less dangerous, more so probably, in the sudden bursting way of a child breaking in from the sidelines, jealous of the play going on around him. He was always there, always behind with the gun and a look on his candlelit face that said nothing at all.

It was the other one who was the leader, the child with ancient eyes. Man One, Charlie called him to himself, and the cyclist he called Man Two.

They gave him a rice ball to eat, twice a day as far as he could tell. He wanted to ask for more but daren't. He was hungry all the time. His stomach yawed and sank inside him and the gastric juices came up and burned the back of his throat.

Two riceballs a day: it was probably all they ate themselves. Not much. No wonder the enemy was so small and so skinny.

Man One and Man Two were small and very skinny. They came and went through the narrow tunnel easily.

Man One asked his name.

"What name?" he asked.

"Charlie."

Man One looked behind him at Man Two and said something Charlie couldn't understand. Man Two's face flickered in the candlelight. He said something quick and angry, jerked his rifle.

"It's my name," said Charlie, looking at the rifle. He wondered what it would sound like, a rifle shot down here. It would spin off the walls and roar. It would deafen him.

"It's my name." He pulled his dog tags out from inside his shirt. "Look. Charlie Lucas. My name."

Man One peered, turning the dog tags this way and that. He cupped his hand behind him and beckoned to Man Two. Man Two put down his rifle and brought the candle closer.

Man One peered again. Charlie could feel his breath on his face. It smelled salty and slightly rancid. The candle was so close now he could feel the heat on his eyeballs. Charlie couldn't tell if Man One was reading the English words or not. He turned to Man Two.

"Chah-ree Ru-cas," he said, and Charlie wanted to cry, hearing his name.

"Chah-ree Ru-cas," said Man Two carefully.

He shuffled back to the entrance of the tunnel and crouched there, the candle in one hand, his rifle across his knees. His face flickered in the candlelight but Charlie couldn't tell anything from it.

Then Man One smiled. He had no teeth in the front at all.

"Chah-ree," he said and laughed, crouched there on his haunches with his knees on each side of his face. "Chah-ree, we have caught him."

He laughed again, flung some words behind him, and Man Two's face flickered a little differently. Charlie thought he was smiling. "Chah-ree we have caught," said Man Two.

Man One said, "You okay, Chah-ree?"

Charlie wanted to cry again. Man One was very kind to him.

"Okay," he said. "Thank you."

He watched Man One's flickering face looking at him from between his knees. No, he wasn't being kind. He was softening him up. For interrogation. He had heard they could be cruel.

"What are you going to do with me?" he asked.

Man One turned his head away and spoke to Man Two. They spoke back and forth. Charlie couldn't understand any of it.

Man One spoke to him. "West. You go west. Soon you go."

"But where am I going?"

"West."

Then they went away. He could hear them jamming in the struts out there in the outer darkness. He wondered which one of them had set the trap that ripped off Lou's head.

He wondered if they got chigger bites.

He lay in the dark and puzzled over it. West was Cambodia. Why would they take him west? A prisoner of war camp? In Cambodia? He'd never heard of one. There was one in Hanoi he'd heard of. The Hanoi Hilton they called it. He'd heard it was bad there. Torture, beatings, electric shocks, death maybe.

But why west?

He lay in the darkness a long time, looking at a map of Indochina behind his eyes.

The Ho Chi Minh Trail. That's what was west.

The Ho Chi Minh Trail up through Cambodia, through Laos. The route to Hanoi. They were taking him to Hanoi. West to Hanoi.

He let the idea sit in his head. West to Hanoi. He couldn't keep it there. It was too big for his head. West to Hanoi. He was weak, ill, half crazy from the darkness, from being alone, from the chigger bites, from the hunger, from the fear. If they beat him he would surely die. On the trail maybe. Certainly in Hanoi. He had nothing to tell them. He was no-one. No-one sitting in a black hole. If they tortured him they would kill him. When they found out he was no-one they would kill him anyway. So Pauline had been right. He was going to die.

But he couldn't think about it. He would lie here in the dark and not think about it.

HOW HE MET PAULINE

He had met Pauline when he was in law school. Her father was an important man around Washington, a diplomat. She had seen a lot of the world because of him and gone to fancy girls' schools in England and Europe. She had poise.

Charlie, on the other hand, was just a down-home boy from Texas who spent most of his life in faded Levis and scuffed cowboy work boots. He had got himself an education, true, but with Pauline he still felt ignorant, and totally unpolished. She was so far above him he couldn't see that high.

He had met her at a party. There were a lot of them around Washington, usually something to do with some politician or somebody's embassy. People went to see and be seen mainly, unless it was a fundraiser, in which case they went to give and be given to, which wasn't so very different. Charlie had no business going to any of them but from time to time one of his schoolmates got in on one, foreigners and people with relatives in high places, and along he would go to see how the other half lived. He avoided fundraisers at all costs.

This particular party was put on by the British. Charlie got there late. He had been observing at a trial and it had gone on a long time and then he hadn't been able to find a parking place on Massachusetts Avenue or any of the nearer back streets. The one he finally found was nearly twenty minutes' walk away. Washington was certainly out and about that night.

Someone he took to be a butler met him at the door and inspected his invitation. Then a waiter with a superior look rejected out of hand the notion of bourbon and branch. He did manage to come up with some Scotch whisky though and Charlie went off clutching the damp glass to look for his friends.

He maneuvered his way through a noisy throng that surged and eddied through the cavernous reception room and spilled out into the room next door where it rushed in urgent little wavelets down the length of a laden banquet table. Charlie had been to enough of these sorts of things by now to have the standard types of party-goers categorized and he assigned them to their boxes as he went.

There were the usual earnest souls in earnest clothes who worked in Capitol Hill offices and went to everything around in the way of receptions and parties. Checked the bosses' invitations, in fact, and used up the ones he turned down. They were the eaters, saving on dinner.

There was a sprinkling of senators and congressmen too, not many, as the opinions of the British ambassador on the most pressing issue of the day—

the war—were not in great demand. But you never know when the British might come in handy, do you? Better go along, meet this man. They were the non-eaters. Can't stuff at all these things. Big waistlines are bad for votes.

There were the people from other embassies, in robes and saris and things on their heads. They pretended to eat, exclaiming over bits and pieces on their plates and moving them around, being polite. They knew from long experience that British cooking is pretty bad but you never know when the British might come in handy, do you?

There were the three-piece men, government officials with combed-across hair and very thin wives. They were even more serious than the people from the Capitol Hill offices: they were working on their careers. Their wives hid whatever it was they were thinking behind polite, agonized smiles. A few didn't even look polite, and one or two seemed very friendly with the drink waiters.

Then there were the usuals. They'd appeared before and would no doubt appear again. They didn't seem to have any particular intentions, were just there. Jocular men who tossed off their laughter with a faintly contemptuous fling. Cerebral men with large heads who talked like people in the know about this important development and that one too, and nodded and held onto their chins. Well-dressed women who seemed to have come alone and not minded a bit, who made it their business to meet everyone in the room and say darling a lot. And, of course, the businessmen, a scattering, with alert eyes and cards announcing their names and status tucked into their vests. Never know who you might meet at one of these things, do you? Everyone needs a congressman in his pocket. Or a senator. Both would be good.

There was another person there that evening, one who didn't fit into any of these categories, standing all by herself in the middle of a space. She was tall, golden of hair and blue of eye. She stood very straight and didn't seem at all disconcerted about being alone.

Charlie broke out of the crowd and made a bee-line for her.

"Hi!" he said.

She looked him directly in the eye and smiled a smile that made him think he was about to have a heart attack.

"Hello," she said in a very proper voice. "I'm Pauline."

She stuck out her hand and it was damp from the drink she had been holding.

Charlie fell in love.

HOW PAULINE CALLED HIM CHARLIE

At first falling in love did him no good at all. He went through some extraordinary plotting and scheming and finally got Pauline to agree to move into the spare room in the house he shared with some other students. But then it turned out that she had agreed to it because she thought it would be a lark to live in a house full of students and made it very clear she had no intention of dating any of them.

"Bad for domestic politics, don't you think?" she said.

Charlie wanted to shout, "Damn domestic politics! I love you!" but he wasn't the type to do something rash like that, so he agreed and loved her secretly in his gentle inoffensive way, never hoping for anything in return. At least he had her around.

In those days he was called Chuck.

"What sort of a name is Chuck?" Pauline said, laughing at him. "Now, Charles—that's a name one can get a grip on."

So she called him Charles.

Later she took to calling him Charlie. The first time she did, it was a frozen December night. He had lit a fire in her little bedroom off the back veranda so that she would be warm when she got home from class. Then he felt anxious about it. Maybe she wouldn't appreciate him going into her room like that.

He hung about on the veranda waiting for her just in case, blowing on his fingers and watching the fire through the window as it sputtered gently to itself in the big old fireplace, casting red shadows about the room.

"Don't mind, do you, Pauline?" he asked out of the shadows behind her when she appeared on the veranda. "Thought you might like a bit of warmth. It's a cold night."

"Oh Charlie, how sweet of you," she said.

After that she always called him Charlie and pretty soon so did everyone else.

He liked to cook and she would help him cut and peel, splashing about in the kitchen sink while he put together one of his famous cook-outs. She would push the golden hair away from her eyes with the back of a wrist, a dripping, mutilated potato in her hand, and look at him and laugh and ask a question in that precise voice of hers; and his heart would stop.

She thought he was a nice chap.

"This is Charlie," she would say, introducing him to a friend. "One of my flatmates. A nice chap."

And he would hold his breath and watch her.

Then everything changed.

It was a hot Washington night and he couldn't sleep. He had left his door open to catch the air and the moonlight came slanting in and fell on the cap and gown flung down on a chair in the corner; he had just graduated from law school.

The moonlight also fell on a letter lying on the bedside table. He had got it two days ago, the same day he graduated. It was from his draft board. Uncle Sam wanted him in Vietnam.

Charlie lay there and sweated and thought about it. He had told no-one yet. He thought about the draft notice and he thought about being a soldier and going away to a strange country and fighting in a war there. He was going to do it. He wondered why.

It wasn't because he was a patriot, although he was that; not because he believed in the war, although he did, in a foggy sort of way; and not because he felt himself forced. He could quite easily have avoided the draft if he'd put his mind to it. But he never had put his mind to it; and until tonight he'd never asked himself why not.

He thought about not doing it. He could still get out of it. It wouldn't be hard. He had the contacts. He thought about what it would be like if he didn't go and suddenly his mind was numbed at the prospect: a whole life of lawyering, one monotonous client after another, one heavily worded legal brief after another, one mournful pin-striped suit after another, until he died of the respectability and dullness of it all.

And he was in love with Pauline and she was unattainable.

Charlie gave up on sleeping. He got out of bed and went outside to the little balcony over the back veranda. There was no wind and the night was breathless.

For a while he stood by the rail and looked at the bright dark sky and the bright silver moon sitting in it. Then he got restless. He made his way down the outside stairway to the veranda near Pauline's room.

There were three wide steps going down from the veranda to a little patch of lawn and in the middle of the lawn was a birdbath with no water and some scraggly weeds growing in it. Charlie sat on the top step and stared at the birdbath. He thought about going away to Vietnam and then he thought about Pauline. He wished she were sitting next to him on the step.

There was a soft sound behind him. He turned. Pauline stood there, her nightgown gleaming white in the moonlight and her hair in her eyes.

"Can't you sleep either, Charlie? Isn't it hot? And so humid."

She rubbed her hands down the sides of her nightgown and Charlie, quite inexplicably, began to cry. He was astonished. He buried his face in his hands.

"Oh, my goodness!" said Pauline and he heard

her bare feet pad across the wooden veranda.

She sat down beside him on the step. "What on earth's the matter, Charlie?"

"I've been drafted."

But that wasn't why he was crying. He was crying because he was in love and she was unattainable and he was going off to be a soldier and maybe he would become a hero and she would change her mind and by then it would be too late because she would already have married someone else.

He took her hand.

After that everything happened so fast it took his breath away.

Without warning, Pauline was in his arms, weeping down his neck, convinced he would die.

"You could be eaten by a tiger over there," she said. "I hear they have them in the jungle. Or you could get some awful tropical disease and rot from the inside out. Or you could get shot, Charlie, or blown up by something. Charlie, you could go over there and never come back."

And then he was in bed with her, making love to her with astonished passion. And then she was crying again.

Pauline never cried. She wasn't the crying type, she of the wry wit and the straight back and the iron control. When she wept like that for him, his heart twisted inside him.

"Marry me, Paul," he said. "I promise I won't

die."

She didn't actually say yes but she did it. He made her a daisy-chain crown to put on her hair and married her down at the local courthouse, and when it was done she took the crown off her own golden hair and put it onto his and then she kissed him and watched him go off to be a soldier. Charlie turned before he went onto his plane and looked back at her, surprised to find himself leaving behind a wife with golden hair and a very straight spine who was convinced he was going to die.

As the plane carried him away from her, Charlie had a strange experience. It was as though he felt his connection to her stretching out like an elastic trail behind him. It became thinner and tauter until it suddenly snapped and flicked back over the horizon.

Not that he stopped loving her; but in some sense his connection to her had broken.

He spent his time at training camp in a kind of vacuum, belonging neither here nor there. But when his feet touched ground in Vietnam and he felt the sudden thrust of the hot dank air in his lungs, he felt as though he had come home. For a moment he was disoriented and then he was home. It was almost as though he had been here before, lived here, belonged here, had been born and raised here, had honored here a long line of ancestors. His hard-won education seemed never to have been. It was as though a new man had been born, as ignorant in his way as the down-home boy he had never quite managed to escape.

He hadn't died as Pauline had predicted. So many had died, but not Charlie. He had clung to his new life, killing and running and hiding and turning into a different person from the one Pauline had kissed and crowned with daisies. While other men counted months and weeks and days, waiting to go home, Charlie just lived his life, killing to stay alive, waiting for what would happen to him.

And then he met Minh.

HOW HE MET MINH

He met her the day Dougherty the truck driver died. Charlie didn't even know what his first name was. He was just Dougherty and he drove a truck.

He took a liking to Charlie, gave him advice, all sorts of advice, about the war, about life in general. He never worried much whether or not Charlie took any of this free wisdom. He just gave it away with a grin and a scratch of the head, pieces of soldier wisdom, like little gifts.

He gave advice about how to keep mosquitoes off.

"You smoke?" he asked Charlie.

Charlie shook his head.

"You better start then." Dougherty nodded sagely. "Best thing for keeping those little devils off. The smoke does it. They don't like smoke. No need to inhale if you don't want to, just hold it in your mouth and puff it around. Keeps them off your face. Nothing worse than getting bitten around the eyes."

Dougherty told him he should always carry a can of Johnson's baby powder in his pack, to prevent crotchrot.

"You keep your balls powdered, you'll be okay," he said. "Dries up the sweat, it does. Works for me."

He told him how to tape the legs of his fatigues to his boots to keep the leeches out.

"Everything here goes for your balls," he said. "Leeches worst of all. You tape your legs, you'll be okay. Rubber bands work too. You'll get those sorry fuckers somewheres else o'course. Belly maybe. They like armpits too. When that happens..." And he told Charlie how to get them off without tearing his skin.

He told him all sorts of other things too. "Charles, my man," he would say when he ran across him. "This here's my second tour and I'll tell you something."

And Charlie, a gentle and tolerant man, would smile his quiet smile and nod. He knew most of this already but he didn't mind.

Dougherty liked him.

"Charles, my man," Dougherty declared one day, squatting in the red dust of the base, watching the air shimmer in the heat, "You don't want to get too serious about this here war, you know."

Charlie smiled.

"Yeah," said Dougherty, shifting from one haunch to the other and flicking a drop of sweat off his chin. "There's more to war than killing gooks, you know."

Charlie turned his head. "What?"

Dougherty winked. "Why having fun of

course. You know. Women. That sort of thing. Making babies." He squirmed his shoulders, looking proud and self-deprecating. "I've made me three to my knowledge, and a raft I don't know about, I'll be bound."

He turned to Charlie and eyed him appraisingly. "Good-looking guy like you, they'd go for you like pigs for shit. They like 'em blond. Believe me, I know." He grinned and shook a cloud of red dust off blond curls that bounced around his ears like a girl's.

Charlie said nothing.

Dougherty screwed up his face and spread his big hands. "Now don't you be looking at me like that, Charles, my man. You need some relaxing."

"I've got a wife back home," said Charlie. "I'm a married man."

There was silence for a while.

"You love this wife?" Dougherty asked.

Charlie nodded, smiling to himself. "Yes."

There was another silence. Dougherty seemed to be struggling with a thought.

"You want to go home to this wife?" he asked at last.

Charlie ran a hand across his stubbly hair and watched the heat dancing in the dust. "That's the plan."

"You want to go home alive?"

"Sure."

"Then you're going to have to relax, my man." Dougherty spoke triumphantly, as though he had the better of some argument. "Let me give you a piece of advice. You get too tense out here, you start to make mistakes. You go out after gooks and you get all tensed up. You come back to base, you gotta relax, get rid of the tension. Otherwise, every time you go out, the tension builds a bit more, and a bit more until finally snap! you're gone—the gooks have got you."

Dougherty slid his eyes sideways at Charlie and rocked back and forth on his heels. "Now, you may not think I know what I'm talking about, me being a driver and not actually going out there any more. But first time round I was out. Damn right I was. Weeks on end. I been there.

"I'm no fool though. They got after me to re-up so I said no more patrols, I done my bit. You let me drive a truck, I'll do it."

He grinned at Charlie. "I like to drive a truck. I'm saving up to buy a rig. For back home. I'm gonna be a trucker. I'm gonna chase that flashing line all over those United States."

He nodded to himself, lost in a private dream.

"Anyways," he went on, "I got eyes in my head. I see what's happening to the guys out there. I see this one and that with the tension building and building and no relief and then one day here I am helping stack those boys in rows. That's what happens when you don't get rid of the tension, Charles, my man. You end up in a nice cozy body bag with flies marching up and down on it trying to figure how to get inside that zipper. Now, you don't want to go back to that pretty little wife of yours in such a condition, do you?"

Charlie couldn't imagine any description of Pauline that could accurately be rendered "pretty little wife," but he laughed and shook his head.

"I'll tell you what," Dougherty went on. "You come with me on my next run into town—I can arrange it, I've got ways—and I'll show you some action. Now, there you go looking at me funny again. You don't have to do nothing you don't feel comfortable with. Just you come along and relax and I'll show you some pretty women. Just looking, eh?" He was cajoling.

And next time Dougherty went into Danang, Charlie, dubious, went along with him.

Charlie looked across the little table of the sidewalk cafe and winked.

"Look what's coming up behind you."

He and Dougherty had been eyeing the local women most of the afternoon, sitting there drinking American beer purloined from some military base and watching, not really lusting, just watching and drinking and watching, making comments and laughing.

This one was more gorgeous than the usual

run of them, and the usual run was gorgeous enough.

"Look what's coming."

"What's coming?" Dougherty twisted his head back to look.

She floated along the street like a vision of an angel seen by a man in hell. Pure white *ao dai* fluttered about her knees and long straight hair the color of night flicked across her face and across the white fabric. She was tiny and slight as a feather and utterly wonderful.

Charlie's stomach lurched. He stared, wanted her to notice him.

There was a crash of flame close behind her that hit the hot fetid air like a rip in the fabric of the universe. She flew toward him on it, arms flung out from her body, white sleeves fluttering against the screaming red backdrop, black hair flying, eyes big and horrified, fixed on him, coming directly at him, spreadeagled on the flaming air.

She missed him though and landed beside him, flat on the ground, the thump of air leaving her lungs drowned by the crash of fire and the screams of stampeding people.

They were running toward him from behind her, running over her. He saw a foot land in the middle of her back, leaving the dirty print of a rubber sandal on the white *ao dai*. He flung himself sideways off his chair, violently, knocking aside the rushing crowd, flinging himself over her body, half kneeling, angrily beating at the deadly legs around them.

He didn't think about what he was doing or what was happening, just acted instinctively, protecting his head, protecting her body, noise loud in his ears drowning out thought, noise echoing from the explosion, the roar of flames, the rush of people, the screaming, the sounds of horror, the sounds of war.

It was silent and he lay across her for a long time, stunned, listening to nothing. He shook his head and pushed himself up on his hands, looking down at the girl underneath him.

She was very still, looked like a rubber toy with all the air gone out of it, looked flat lying there on the ground with her black hair singed and full of dirt.

He touched her shoulder gently. "Ma'am, it's okay now. You're okay."

She was lying face down with her head turned to one side, resting with her cheek against the ground. He couldn't see her face. Her black hair fell thickly, hiding it. He brushed it back gently, just one finger, not wanting to presume by touching.

"Ma'am? You okay? You've got to wake up now. It's all done. Time to go home."

She didn't move. He put his face close to hers, listening for her breathing. "Oh, God," he whispered. "Let her be alive. Don't let her be dead, God."

She was breathing.

He turned to Dougherty. "Hey, Dougherty, she's breathing. Give me a hand here to get her up, will you?"

He came up into a crouch and looked up at Dougherty, grinning with relief. "She's going to be okay, Dougherty. How about that?"

The little table was on its side, one leg sticking out and splintered. Dougherty was spread across it, his head hanging down and his backside stuck up in the air. There was a big hole in him at about the kidneys and blood was running down from it onto the back of his head, gathering in the tumbled golden curls and dripping, one slow drop at a time, into the dust.

Charlie stood up slowly, moving like a very old man. He could see pieces of vertebra in the hole in Dougherty's back, all broken around. He stared at it, like at a living thing. Then he bent double, fell to his knees, and threw up in the dust. Dougherty's blood ran down into the vomit.

"What did you go and do that for, Dougherty? What did you have to go and die for? You were supposed to show me a good time."

He watched the blood pooling down and he watched the line of red saliva hanging from the corner of his mouth. It grew long and thin and when it had stretched out long enough to mix with the pooled blood and the vomit he shook his head and spat and wiped his mouth hard against the sleeve of his jacket.

He turned to the girl and gently stroked the thick black hair down over her face, hiding her eyes from the sight.

"It's okay," he said. "It's okay now."

Then he got up off the ground, pushing against the trembling in his knees, eased Dougherty's body down off the table, and laid it on its back. He crossed the arms over the chest and closed the horrified eyes.

"It's okay, fella. Just you rest there a while now. I'm going to take the lady home. You just wait right here for me, you hear?"

The girl was slight but her dead weight was heavy. He moved her across the street out of the sun, under the overhanging roof of a store. He propped her there and crouched beside her, rubbing her wrists and stroking her face, feeling dazed, not able to think what to do next.

She opened her eyes suddenly, impaling him on her terror, and her delicate fingers fluttered around her face like disoriented birds.

"It's okay, ma'am, okay." Charlie crooned the words, nothing in his mind but calming the fright and horror out of her eyes. "Okay, okay, now."

His body rocked gently with the words but he dared not put his hands on her again, not now that she was conscious, looking at him like that, not daring to intrude on her.

The fluttering subsided and the fear gradually went away to the back of her eyes where it hid itself, not gone, just waiting for next time. She spoke, her voice fluttering up and down like her hands had done before. She was asking a question.

Charlie nodded down at her, and smiled. "It's okay now, ma'am, okay," he said again. He had a sudden urgent need to take her in his arms and rock her with the words. "Okay, okay, now." But he didn't, just smiled gently down at her, making his face soft and unthreatening and soothing, rocking his body back and forth.

She struggled to sit up.

He reached for her elbow to help her but she pulled away. She shook her head and eased herself up into a sitting position against the flimsy wood of the storefront, propping herself on each side, her hands flat on the ground.

Charlie eased himself out of her way, squatting beside her on his haunches.

"I will help you," he said, mouthing slowly as if that would help her to understand the foreign words. "Help." He pointed to himself and to her, and mimed a picking up action.

She shook her head, watching his eyes care- ʼv. Then she folded her knees underneath herself, ·t stage upwards. Her eyes were concentrated inward now, as if examining each part of herself to see if it would still function. She seemed satisfied with what she found, pushed her hair back from her face and looked at him, unsmiling.

"Okay," she said firmly. "Minh is okay."

"You speak English then?" Charlie peered at her, trying to see into her mind. What was she thinking? How was she feeling? Did she hate him for this? Hate the Yankee intruder?

He pointed to himself again. "American. GI. I will help you."

Some of the distrust slid away from her eyes. She smiled, ever so faintly. "GI Joe," she said. "Hello Joe."

"Hello Minh." He pointed to himself again. "I am Charlie."

She looked at him intently, a quizzical flicker at the corner of her mouth. "Charlie I know," she said. "Victor Charlie. VC. Why you call Charlie?"

"Sometimes Charlie's the good guy," he said.

HOW MINH'S FATHER DIDN'T THINK
HE WAS A GOOD GUY

Charlie was besotted. He couldn't get Minh off his mind. Her slim form wound itself through his dreams and he constantly came upon her as they rampaged their way through one *ville* after another looking for Viet Cong. She was always the tiny girl running away from him.

He knew none of these fleeting pixies was her but every time he saw one his heart would spring into his throat and he would catch at himself to stop from chasing after it, cursing himself for a fool.

He tried not to go back into Danang and for a long time he succeeded.

But it got worse. He became dazed with desire. He narrowly missed death on several occasions and it was nothing but inattention. He began to make up excuses in his mind about Pauline.

She was not the one for him after all, he told himself. He should never have married her. It was a mistake. He only did it because he had been taken by surprise; because she was suddenly available and he'd never dreamed she would be. He did it just to show himself that he could have her.

And she hadn't really wanted him. She had done it only because she had pitied him. After all, she had been convinced that he would die so what was to be lost? Certainly it was just pity. She had no lasting feeling for him.

Charlie became angry. It had been heartless on her part, leading him on like that.

He thought of how they had made love. It had all been on his side, he told himself. She had been cold, wooden. Looking back it was all so obvious. She was heartless, a cool, practical woman with no passion in her.

He hadn't noticed at the time because of his own excitement. But it hadn't been love. It had only been animal lust. And fear. He hadn't admitted it to himself then but the fear had been there. Making love to Pauline had taken it away. It had given him a reason to come back.

"Charlie, you might die over there," she had said. And she'd cried, pitying him. She had pitied him and let him make love to her. She had let him marry her.

But to pity him was not heartless, was it?

No, but she was cruel in that. If she had let him make love to her and let it be then it would have been an act of kindness. But then she had married him. That was an act of cruelty.

He remembered how she had looked waving him goodbye, so tall and straight, and such a sad, serious face. Already regretting her hastiness, no doubt.

She wrote to him regularly, true, but that was because she now felt an obligation. Her letters were cold and stilted, a dead giveaway. She told him about the weather and about the neighbors. She told him about school and that damn fool of a philosopher she was studying. What was his name? He couldn't remember. As if he cared about some dead philosopher anyway. She never told him she longed for him. She never told him she lay awake nights dreaming of his touch.

But of course she didn't. She was trying to figure out a way to rid herself of him. She sat every day with a pencil and that lined yellow pad she always used and drafted letters telling him she had made a mistake, that she didn't really love him, that she would like to end it all discretely. Then she tore them up. Not because she didn't plan to send one in the end but because she hadn't got one worded to her liking yet.

She was very proper. She wouldn't send one until she had every nuance just right. When it came it would be clear without being blatant, final without being ruthless.

Dear Charlie, it would say, *sorry to have to tell you this but . . .*

He had seen other men get letters like that. It was a humiliation. And he could do nothing about it. All he could do was wait and there it would be.

He decided he wouldn't let her humiliate him.

And after he had decided that he began to see things more clearly. He saw that she didn't have it in her power to humiliate him after all. She could only humiliate him if he loved her. But he didn't love her. It had all been a mistake on his part. He'd made it up.

When he thought about it some more he realized that he hadn't really married her at all, now had he? He'd misremembered. That was it. He'd been confused and misremembered.

And so he built up a wall in his mind. Brick by brick he built it, reasoning it all out to himself. The higher it got the less he could see Pauline. He built it up past her long straight legs and her long straight back and her long straight hair. He built it so high that after a while he couldn't see over the top any more. Her letters became like communications from the moon. He stopped reading them. He stopped writing to her.

And all the time he was dazed with passion for Minh.

One day he went into Danang. He remembered how he had taken Minh home the day Dougherty got blown up. The route to her house was as clear in his mind as if he held a map.

He made his way slowly through the shouting, crowded streets, telling himself as he went that this was a bad idea and then telling himself that it was the best idea he ever had. Once he came upon a group of stoned Marines. One of them called out to him but he turned his face away and picked up his pace. When he looked back over his shoulder they were gone. He slowed again, matching his pace to the back and forth inside his head.

He came to her street. It was hot and dusty and dense with bodies. Bicycles and little putt-putting motorbikes flooded up and down and street vendors stared curiously at him as he made his way. They turned and talked to each other, darting furtive glances after him and straining their necks to see where he was bound.

A little boy wearing nothing but a torn gray undershirt stopped in front of him.

"Hi, Joe," he said and held out his hand. He still had the pot belly of a baby but his eyes were wise.

Charlie smiled at him and shook his head. The child wandered off, phlegmatic.

He came to her house. It wasn't much of a house, a plain affair of clapboard and very small, jammed up between houses just as humble. But to Charlie it was the castle of a princess. He knew he had done the right thing coming.

She didn't seem surprised to see him. It was almost as if she had been expecting him. She took him inside to show to her mother.

Charlie looked around at his princess' castle. He told himself he could live in a place like this if

Minh were there.

There was only one room and the floor was a concrete slab. The cooking area was at the back and there was a ragged curtain, like an old sheet, pulled halfway across in front of it. On the left wall was a ladder that vanished into a squarish hole in the ceiling. He assumed that was where the family went to sleep.

Where he stood just inside the door there were some low stools set on a rush mat. It had been red once with a green pattern running through it. There was a tarnished fat-bellied kettle set between two of the stools. Off to the right, between the rush mat and the hanging curtain, was a big old black Singer sewing machine. Charlie had seen such machines in museums. It had a hinged metal platform underneath for pumping the needle. There was no electricity here apparently.

Beside the sewing machine a big basket overflowed with colored pieces of fabric and on the floor there was a sheet of clear plastic with two halves of a brilliant yellow *ao dai* spread out flat on it like a person sliced neatly in half and set out in the sun to dry.

Minh's mother was sitting at the sewing machine, darting thread into the eye of the needle. She rested her hands against the top of the machine and heaved herself to her feet.

"American, yes?" she said and grinned.

Charlie was surprised by her. Minh was slight and delicate and beautiful but this woman was stout and plain. Her teeth were black from chewing betel and she spat between them from time to time, pinging long jets of saliva into the fat-bellied kettle. She was nothing but a fat ignorant peasant, not a fitting mother for a princess.

But she welcomed him and had him sit on a low stool while she went to the back of the room and made a commotion with some blackened pots there. She brought him *pho* and grinned and said, "Ai-ee! American! Very good!" And watched him drink it, moving her mouth to taste it with him.

"Okay?" she asked anxiously when Charlie had blown on the hot liquid and managed to cool it enough to take some into his mouth. "Okay?"

Minh sat at his feet on the rush mat. Charlie smiled at her. Then he smiled at her mother. "Okay," he said. "Very good."

He felt at home here. He was very comfortable drinking *pho* and basking in Minh's presence. Her mother was not so bad after all. He wished she would leave them alone just for a moment but he knew she wouldn't and it didn't really matter.

Minh and her mother spoke French as well as Vietnamese and a little English. Minh had more English than her mother. She had been to classes, she said, and her father spoke some English too.

"Father come soon," she said after a while. "You go now. Come back next day."

Charlie thought nothing of it. He came back the next day he could, and the next, and the next. And soon he seemed to become part of the family. Sometimes he felt as though he had always belonged here, as though he had known Minh forever.

He was very comfortable.

One day Minh's mother left them alone. It was as though he had passed some test. They made love that day. It was very easy. Minh was not at all shy. She simply shut the door behind her mother and came into his arms and they lay down together on the floor, right there on the rush mat, and made love.

When he was getting ready to leave, Minh's mother appeared again as if by magic.

"Very good, yes?" she asked. "Okay?"

Charlie felt a queasiness pass by him but it was gone in a moment. He was too happy and too besotted by Minh and too satisfied. He smiled at Minh and then at her mother.

"Very good," he said. "Okay."

"You come back next day?" asked Minh's mother anxiously.

"Of course. As soon as I can. Of course." He kissed Minh and didn't mind at all the little clicking sounds of approval her mother made.

After that, he came every time he could get

away. He told no-one where he was going and took no-one with him to Minh's house. He had never been a talker and so he didn't find his secret hard to keep. He hugged it to himself. He smiled about it privately. And he was very careful not to get killed.

He worried, though, about being seen with her. He didn't want it to get around. He wasn't ashamed, he told himself. It just wasn't anyone's business but his. So he didn't take her out much, especially not to places where there might be other Americans.

Minh didn't seem to mind. It even seemed to Charlie that she had her own reasons for not going out in public with him. He was right about that, as it turned out, but for the longest time everything fell into a happy pattern of privacy and love-making.

This happy domesticity was shattered the day Minh's father appeared on the scene. He came home unexpectedly. Fortunately, Charlie had just arrived and Minh's mother had not yet gone off to wherever it was she went on these occasions so the situation was not too compromising.

He was one of the tiniest men Charlie had ever seen: less than five feet tall and slight as a breeze, like Minh. His wife loomed enormous by comparison.

He had something wrong with his left foot. It was twisted and misshapen. He walked on it with difficulty and when he stood still his body listed to one side. But his small size and his lameness were offset by his ferocity. He bristled and glowered at Charlie like a terrier who has just seen a rat.

Minh's mother spoke first, and there was a swift altercation. She seemed undaunted by her husband's wrath, although Charlie couldn't tell who was getting the better of the argument.

When all the words had been said, Minh's father turned to Charlie and his face showed nothing.

"Go away, American," he said, and the emotion was all in his voice.

Then he stalked out of the house with his twisted foot banging angrily against the floor.

Minh's mother watched him go. She turned to Charlie and rolled up her eyes and spread her hands out with the palms upwards.

"That one not like American," she said and laughed. "You come next day?"

And so an arrangement was worked out. Minh's mother would stand watch when he came. More than once she sent a small boy running to bang on the door and warn the lovers, but it was always in time. Charlie thought nothing of it. It was a family conspiracy. It was fun.

He was curious, though, about Minh's father. He asked her about him.

At first she just smiled. "No worry," she said. "Mother like American. Is okay. No worry. You good guy."

"Your father doesn't seem to think I'm a good guy. Why doesn't he like Americans?"

Minh made a little apologetic movement with her hands. She didn't want to talk about it.

Charlie began to worry.

He developed a nagging feeling that Minh's father might be Viet Cong. If not that, then at least a communist sympathizer. He began to go over in his mind the repercussions this might have on him. Could this be classed as consorting with the enemy? Would he one day find himself branded as a traitor? How could he find out? Ask Minh? If it were not true she might reject him.

He became tormented by doubts. Perhaps she didn't love him at all. Perhaps she was a trap set and waiting for an unwitting American to fall into and be ruined.

At last he could bear it no longer. He asked her point blank and waited for the anger and recriminations.

She was reluctant at first but he pressed her and she laughed with her hand in front of her teeth. *"Nationaliste,"* she said. "He is *nationaliste* only."

Charlie was confused. "But how can being a nationalist make him hate Americans? We're trying to help you get back your country."

But Minh wanted to make love and so there was no more talking that day.

HOW HE CAME TO UNDERSTAND
MINH'S FATHER

Minh did talk about her father eventually. It didn't come in a flood or an orderly conversation, just bit by bit over time.

He didn't hate Americans only, she told him. He hated the French too.

"But the French are long gone now."

Minh lifted her shoulders. He hated them still.

She didn't remember the French herself. She had been a tiny baby when they had been thrown out. She spoke their language but she didn't remember them at all.

"Were they very bad?"

She supposed they were. They took over Vietnam and made the Vietnamese people serve them. Her father had hated them. Her grandfather too, although she didn't remember him. She remembered stories though, of how the *nationalistes* would hunt the French secretly in the streets and kill them. One at a time and cruelly they did it: a knife low in the belly, a bullet in the spine, a quick shove into the river and a stick to hold the struggles under the water.

"Your father did these things?"

She didn't know. She had heard stories only. Everyone had hated the French. And they had beaten them in the end, at Dien Bien Phu.

"What about your father's foot. What happened to it?"

It was the communists did that, Minh told him. They had accused her grandfather of something. Charlie couldn't get it clear what. Her grandfather wouldn't confess so they had tortured his son to make him. But he had watched them smash his son's ankle with a rock and still he had refused. He had cursed them, in Vietnamese and in French too. His son had been crippled ever since and never held it against his father.

He held it personally against Ho Chi Minh though. He hated Ho Chi Minh because he had betrayed the *nationalistes* to the French in order to gain control of them. He hated all communists. He hated the Viet Cong and the northern communists and the Russians too because they were trying to make a colony out of Vietnam. And the Chinese because they had always tried to and would try again. He hated everyone who had ever threatened Vietnamese independence. He was a *nationaliste* like his father and his grandfather before him.

Charlie thought about all this for three weeks. He shot four men and a stampeding buffalo in that time. He felt fear but no animosity towards any of them. It had to be done, even the buffalo.

"But America is no threat," he said to Minh the next time he was with her. He had his face in her hair. It smelled of new rain. "We're trying to help your country."

Apparently Minh's father didn't want America's help.

Charlie went back and shot some more people while he thought about it again. He couldn't remember how many he shot that time but when it was done he thought he understood Minh's father right enough. Such a bitter nationalist would just naturally resent help from America. In the same way, a small boy would resent his big brother taking up for him in a fight he could not win on his own. It robbed him of his dignity. And being crippled wouldn't help.

Charlie found a sneaking sympathy for such pride. And it certainly relieved his worries about being accused of collaborating with the Viet Cong. It didn't help his personal situation though. He still had to sneak in and out of Minh's house like a thief.

Her father began to prey on his mind in a different way. Now he felt he was giving him reason to hate Americans, deceiving him like this. Minh was his daughter, after all, his only child. He would try to make friends with the man, he resolved, now that he understood him.

But Minh and her mother both were horrified

at the idea. As for his understanding, it wasn't relevant. They just looked blank at his protestations and he felt embarrassed after all.

What arrogance, he told himself as he tramped through the graveyard and down the path of yet another *ville* to chase the people out of their hooches and maybe kill some of them too, to claim he understood anyone in this country. How could he understand a man who had been tortured so badly? How could he understand anyone who had to go through life with his foot twisted backwards? Someone who didn't blame his father for being the cause of it. In America a man would blame his father for something like that. People blamed their fathers for much less all the time. Charlie felt ashamed.

He didn't shoot anyone that day. The *ville* was clean.

HOW MINH'S MOTHER MADE A GOOD LIFE
FOR HER DAUGHTER

"He hates them all," said Minh's mother. "The Japanese. The British."

Minh had come to the end of what she knew. Charlie's curiosity was too much for her. She had persuaded her mother to talk to him.

The Japanese, yes, Charlie could understand that. He knew about the Japanese. Coming in and taking over the country the way they had, it was understandable to hate them.

"But the British? Why on earth the British? What did they ever do to Vietnam?"

There was a commotion in the street outside and Minh's mother heaved herself to her feet. She went to the door and looked out. There was the sound of running and then a lot of voices. She joined in enthusiastically.

When it was all settled to her satisfaction she came back and lowered herself onto her stool. She set her feet apart and balanced her weight carefully. She spoke to Charlie but she looked at Minh. She had given up on English for today. It was too many words.

Minh got ready to interpret. She tipped her

head on one side and moved her mouth when her mother spoke. It was as though she was taking the words from her mother's mouth into her own.

"The British gave us back to the French when the Japanese fell." Minh's mother shifted her wad of betel from her right cheek to her left and chewed a while, meditatively.

"The Japanese were not so bad," she went on. "They did not want to have our country for themselves. They just used it for a while. They put the French in jail. They let us govern ourselves.

"The *nationalistes* were very happy at that time. We had our emperor still and we had our independence. My husband was full of energy. He did not care about his leg any more. He went to many meetings. He dreamed. He was young. All the young men dreamed great dreams for their country in those days. And the women too.

"We lived in the north at that time. We were not poor there. My husband's father owned land. He was a farmer. And my father also. But then the Japanese fell down and the British let the French out of jail."

Charlie interrupted her. "But I still don't understand. Why the British?"

She spoke directly to him then while Minh took her words and spoke the English for them softly. She was always a little behind, like a following echo.

"They came to help with the peace." Minh's

mother looked at Charlie as a schoolteacher might at a boy who has not learned his lesson. "But they betrayed us also to the French. They let them out of jail and gave them guns. What could we do? My husband fought them, and his friends too. Many people altogether fought. Ho Chi Minh was the leader then. And no-one talked of communism. No-one cared about it. We cared for nothing but Vietnam's independence. I fought too. I was a fighter in those days."

Minh's mother laughed, showing her black teeth. She took aim and spat. It made a sharp ringing sound on the fat-bellied kettle. Charlie wanted to turn his eyes away but she watched him and he dared not do it.

"The communists betrayed us also in the end. Bit by bit they did it. It was because we were not communists and they wanted to take the power. They stole away in the night and told our positions to the French. That was a time of great confusion. Some people grew so angry with the communists' treachery that they joined the French to fight against them. It seemed that everyone was fighting everyone. The communists planned it that way. In the confusion they killed many, many people. They killed off the leaders of the non-communist *nationalistes* so that we could not stand against them. The French helped them do it. Oh, it was a grand slaughter."

Minh's mother spat again. Her eyes had gone a long way off. She sat on her stool with her knees spread and her feet set squarely. They were the feet of a stubborn woman.

She sucked in her breath in a little hissing rush and started again.

"My own father, he was murdered. And many others. All the intellectuals. All the leaders. My own father. I saw it. I hid in the trees and I saw it happen. They knocked him down and dragged him to the river. I followed, hiding in the trees. I was alone and big in my belly. There was no-one to help.

"There were many others by the river. The communists had captured them. They lay on the ground—twenty, thirty maybe.

"They had sacks and they put them in. Two men went from sack to sack and sewed up the tops. Then they threw them in the river, dead or alive I do not know, but then they drowned. Some of them sank and some ran off on top of the river.

"One I saw struggling on top of the river. Inside the sack he was not dead. I heard him cry out. I think it was not my father but how could I tell? He struggled and then he went under the water."

She gathered her spittle again and aimed at the kettle. Her eyes were flat and dark as stones.

"That night I had my child. I never had another. It was the fear. It twisted up inside my belly so I could not bear again."

She tipped her head side to side and stretched her mouth into a line. "My husband does not love me now because I have no sons. A daughter only."

Charlie looked at Minh but she was watching her mother with no expression.

"And after that?"

"I was ill after that. I did not see the French fall. I was sorry for that. My husband was not there either. He could not walk. He was still recovering from his injury. He was very angry not to be there."

Minh's mother was tiring of her story. She pushed her hands flat against her knees and stood up.

"Soon we ran away to the south. We could not stay with the communists. It was too dangerous. We came to Danang."

She made a sound of disgust at the back of her throat. "We left all our family behind. Now we do not know if they are dead or alive. And after all it was no good. The Americans, they helped Diem and they put the French sympathizers into power in the government. After that there was no strength left in the *nationaliste* movement."

"And your husband?"

"A madman. He fights with phantoms. He earns no money. We are poor and sometimes we have no food and he meets with his friends and they are all madmen together."

"But Diem is gone now."

"And now he hates the Americans."

She went to her ancient sewing machine and

sat down behind it. For a while the only sound was the rattle of her sewing.

Charlie said nothing. He had been surprised again by Minh's mother. He had taken her for an ignorant peasant. But he had judged her wrong. This woman was no ignorant peasant. She understood many things. Her father had been an intellectual.

He watched her sew. Her feet pumped up and down, up and down. She clattered her way down one side of a pale pink *ao dai*. She broke the thread, turned the fabric up the other way, and clattered down the other side. She broke the thread again. Then she stood up with the garment in her hand and shook it. She held it away from her and inspected her work.

"As for me, I stay at home and make clothes," she said, looking closely at a pucker in one seam. "I was sick after my daughter was born."

She took hold of the fabric on each side of the pucker and pulled it sharply. There was a snapping sound of thread breaking. She sat down again at her machine, rattled along the offending section, broke the thread and stood up to inspect it again.

"For a long time I was sick and very weak. But I had to make clothes to feed us because even then my husband made little money. He was busy with his dreams and his meetings. So I made myself a little business. I sewed and I took care of my daughter."

She smiled at Minh and, still holding the *ao dai* in one hand, came over to touch her hair. She loved her daughter greatly.

Then she went back to her sewing machine and laid the soft pink silk over it, setting it down carefully. She turned to Charlie and began to speak again.

Next to him Charlie heard Minh clear her throat with a soft puff of air. She followed after her mother's words.

"Vietnam is doomed. We are a foolish people. We lose and lose and everyone marches on us. It will not change. And inside me I am still sick. There is something growing in my belly. It is very big now. It makes me swell."

She held her hands out wide, like a fisherman boasting of his catch.

"So I will die and not care any more about the *nationalistes*. I will make good life for my daughter and then I will die and not care."

Uneasiness turned in Charlie's stomach. He turned his face to Minh. "How will you do that?" he asked her mother.

"I will give her to you." Minh spoke her mother's words very softly. Her eyes were pleading. "You are very good man. Kind. Rich. You will take her to America. I do not care if my husband hates the American. It is good life there. Many people say it. My daughter will be good wife. I have sent her to school. She can speak English. She knows many things. Yes, she will be very good wife for you, I think. She will have sons and her husband will not be a madman. He will be American husband, yes?"

Minh's voice was like a bird calling to its mate. Her eyes bewitched him. The smell of her hair robbed him of his reason.

Don't be a fool, man.

He couldn't help himself. "I would be proud to have her as my wife."

That was how it happened. It seemed he had proposed. Her mother arranged for a secret wedding. She went to the Catholic priest and arranged it. He was happy to have the new converts.

And Minh's father would never hear of it from a priest. He would have nothing to do with priests. He hated them all. They had been bred by the French and their religion was the religion of France. He hated the French because they had brought opium to Vietnam and destroyed the people's brains; then they had stolen their souls and offered them up to a foreign, bloody god. No, Minh's father would never learn anything from a priest.

And so they were married. Minh glowed with happiness, her mother with triumph. She had made a good life for her daughter; now she could die and not care.

Charlie added another layer of bricks to the wall in his mind, making it higher, a tall barrier between Minh and Pauline, between Vietnam and

America. And when he realized that his time was short he re-enlisted and made it long again.

HOW MINH CALLED HIS SON CHARLIE

It turned out that Minh had been pregnant when he married her. She hadn't told him and it was months before her waist grew thick. When he finally noticed it, someone inside Charlie's head began to talk to him, telling him that he was in deep trouble here.

Minh told him breathless tales about her father. He did not know his daughter had married the American but he knew where this baby had come from. He was accusing and ashamed. He cursed Charlie and insisted that Minh get an abortion.

But her mother tricked him.

She hid Minh for a day and a night and told her husband that the abortion had been done. By the time he discovered the truth, it was too late.

When Charlie heard this, the voice inside his head said it would have been better if they had really done it, but he tried not to listen.

Then Minh reported that her father had taken to calling the child American half-breed. He spat on the ground at her feet. He refused to speak directly to her. He talked to himself and to the air around him. He threatened to drown the child when it was born. He threatened Charlie's life if he should ever catch him near her again. He hired a boy to watch the house. He was to run and tell him if an American came.

Minh's mother hired the same boy. She paid him more than her husband. She threatened his genitals if he should try to play both sides.

Charlie became afraid to visit. When he did, he had to listen to more stories from Minh and her mother about how they had tricked her father. They were proud of it. They laughed together about it.

Charlie felt bad about this. The voice inside his head told him that he had been tricked by them himself; he had been taken for a sucker. He refused to admit to that, but he could see that he had indeed gotten himself into very deep trouble.

He came less often, making excuses. He did not make love to Minh any more and he wished he hadn't re-upped; he had been a fool. His mind whirled and whirled, trying to figure out what to do.

Pauline began to wander at the edges of his consciousness.

One day it occurred to Charlie that Pauline would be expecting him back soon so he wrote to her at last and told her that he'd re-upped.

I've re-upped, he said; just like that, with no explanation.

He knew that she had got his letter because she didn't answer, not for a long, long time.

He imagined her, with her long golden hair

and her long legs, standing very straight and holding his letter in her hand. She read it without saying a word. Then she called her mother.

"It seems that Charlie has re-enlisted," she said in her proper voice.

She was holding the phone up to her ear with her left hand. In her right she held his letter.

"Odd, that," she said.

Then she didn't answer, not for a long, long time.

And in that time, Minh had her baby. Charlie became a father.

"What to call your son?"

Minh held the child out to him and smiled. It was small and dark, a tiny oriental face.

Charlie stared down at it, horrified. Minh's father had called it American half-breed but it didn't look like a half-breed to Charlie. There was nothing of America in this scowling little face. This was the face he hunted through the dripping jungle. This was the face of the enemy. His son, the enemy.

Charlie had a strange disconnected feeling. It occurred to him that he had been hunting his own flesh and blood through the jungle all this time.

Minh nudged the little bundle into his arms. "What to call?" she asked again.

"You tell me," he said. "What is his name?"

"Charlie. His name is Charlie, after his father."

Charlie let out his breath in a long, soft moan and she looked up at him quickly.

"But that is for America. He also must have Vietnamese name. He will be Vuong. It is good Vietnamese name. He will use it here only. When we go to America he will be Charlie. American name for American boy. Here he will be Vietnamese." She moved her head side to side just slightly. "Is better that way."

She stopped, leaving something unsaid.

Charlie had an urgent feeling that it was something important but he couldn't think what it might be.

"I will have new name also in America," Minh went on, watching his face. "I will be Marilyn Monroe."

Charlie laughed anxiously. "That name's already taken. It would be bad luck."

He thought a moment. "How about Michelle? That's a pretty name."

But she was adamant. "No. It is French. I will have American name. Not French."

"How about Mary Lou, then? That's a good American name. You like that?"

Minh smiled. "Mary Lou . . ." She tried it out on her tongue. "I like."

She began to plan her life in America where her son would be an American boy and she would have a Mixmaster and learn to make down-home cooking because that was what Charlie liked. She would be an American lady. She would be rich and have very good jeans.

Charlie listened to her plans and said nothing. After a while he realized that she really believed in this new life she dreamed of. He was indeed in very serious trouble.

He still told no-one about her. He went to see her from time to time and held his son, looking down into his face with bewilderment: Charlie the Charlie.

Charlie. The enemy. Little slant-eyed devils that crept after you, hiding from you, watching you from places you couldn't find, springing out on you to kill you in the end.

He began to fear his son.

And then Pauline wrote. She didn't mention him re-upping, not a word about it. No exclamations, no recriminations, no pleas. Just told him the news and that was it.

A strange letter. What if he told her he had a son? Would she write and tell him the news as though he'd never mentioned it?

She wrote regularly again after that, every seven days as before. At first he still read her letters as though they were letters from the moon, as though they had nothing to do with him; but with each one another brick loosened on the wall in his mind.

He thought about Pauline. Sometimes he wanted to abandon her. But then he would remember how her hair was blond like his and her eyes were like his too, round and blue. He remembered how he could look straight into her eyes without bending his knees or making her turn up her face. He remembered how she stood very straight and spoke with a proper accent, every word perfectly articulated. He never had to ask her to repeat because she got her words mixed up or couldn't find the right one. He remembered how he had understood everything perfectly; and he remembered how comfortable it was to understand perfectly like that.

He thought about Minh too. He imagined what it would be like to take her home to meet Pauline. Pauline would be very civilized. She would stand very straight and Minh would have to turn up her face to see so high.

"How do you do?" Pauline would say and put out her hand.

Minh would be holding his son on her back and she would not have a hand to offer. She would giggle in embarrassment.

Pauline would pat the child's hand, giving Minh back her face. "And how do *you* do?" she would say.

Oh yes, she would be very civilized.

Then they would all four go out together.

"Meet my wives," Charlie would say, running across an acquaintance. "And meet my son."

"How do you do?" Pauline would say in her proper accent but Minh's words would all fly into the air and fall back down in some extraordinary pattern. The child would glower over her shoulder.

The acquaintance would look at his wives and the sour face of his son and hurry away.

"Never mind," Pauline would say. "Off we go."

She would lead the way and Charlie would come behind leading Minh by the hand. The child would turn its head on her shoulder and look at its father with dark foreign eyes.

Charlie began to feel trapped. Minh and her mother had trapped him with the child. He felt used. He was nothing more than a ticket to America. His fear of the child grew and resentment grew with it. He became angry, and he felt guilty about his anger.

All this emotion he funneled into reckless bravery. Whereas before he had killed because he was a soldier, now he became a killer: Charlie, the Charlie killer. He became fierce and thin. He hunted the enemy ruthlessly and killed him savagely. He counted the bodies afterwards with atavistic glee. He cut off the ears and strung them around his neck. He lusted for scalps.

For a long time he was a wild jungle animal,

thinking only of killing, but then he began to feel schizophrenic. He hated the enemy and he hated himself. He hated the child he had bred. And before long every dead Charlie became his son, every limp body his own flesh, every rush of blood his.

It was not long after that they took away his ears. They said he'd burned out. But he hadn't, not really. He just couldn't do it any more. He had exhausted himself with killing his son.

HOW THEY SAID HE'D BURNED OUT

It happened the day he killed the sniper.

It had been a terrible night, alive and screaming with battle. The ground heaved and shook and the air thundered around them, full of dust and smoke and the smell of men's terror. Many died before the morning dragged itself out of the mist and the clouds of smoke and sent the enemy back into the earth and the planes off into the sky and silenced it all.

Then out of the silence someone started to sing. He had a full, deep voice and he sang with all his heart, belting it out like a teary-eyed patriot before a ball game. The sound went rolling out across the valley and echoed back in its own refrain:

> Oh, say can you see,
> By the dawn's early light,
> How we ripped up their ass
> From the twilight's first gleaming?
> Yeah, we showered down shit
> Through the perilous night,
> O'er the ramparts we crapped
> Till the assholes were screaming.
> And the rocket's red glare,
> The bombs bursting in air,

Blew the balls off the dinks,
Fuckers ain't got a prayer...

The singer trailed off into a loud humming and cheering broke out along the line of men. When it had died away there was silence in the jungle for the space of half a minute.

Then there he was, the sniper, up in a tree, picking away at them from behind it with whistling single shots. He must have been up there all night.

Charlie caught his sergeant's eye and jerked his head towards the tree. The sergeant kept his head down but he raised his hand a couple of inches off the ground and made a circle with his thumb and fore-finger.

Charlie cradled his rifle in his elbows and belly-walked his way in a wide arc through the undergrowth to the back of the tree. There, he raised the rifle, aimed, and got him. He waited for him to come tumbling out of the tree but only his rifle fell. The sniper stayed there, all flopped around, hanging up there like a scarecrow.

Charlie came back to the others and they all crouched around and stared up the tree, watching the dead sniper sway above them.

The sergeant broke the silence. He was a nuggetty man with a broken nose. "Let's get him down from there. See what he's got on him." He looked at Charlie. "He's your bag. You get him."

So Charlie slung his rifle across his back and climbed the tree, trying not to think about the other trees around or the gun sights that could right now be on him or where the bullet might hit. If it came he hoped he'd hear it. They said you never hear the one that kills you. He hoped he'd hear it.

He came up underneath and twisted his neck until he could see the sniper's arms dangling above him, and his head hanging down with the hair falling away from it as though it were standing up in fright. He had tied himself to the tree by a piece of vine, wrapping it around his waist and securing the end so he wouldn't have to hold on, so he could aim and fire and aim and fire and not fall.

And he hadn't, not even when he was dead. The hands that had worked the rifle hung limp and helpless off the ends of his arms. They were small hands, like a child's.

Charlie felt his throat go tight. He shook his head. He had seen them dead before. This one was just another.

But something worked inside him. A choking sob started deep down below his diaphragm and fought its way up the back of his throat. Tears sprang behind his eyes.

He scrambled to the back of the trunk, jerked out his knife and hacked through the vine, watching as the little man fell down past him, bounced twice off branches and flopped onto the ground. He looked flat and broken from up in the tree.

Charlie began to cry.

"Come on now. Come on now. Come on now."

He said it over and over to himself but it didn't do any good. He clung to the tree and cried and cried and couldn't stop.

The others crouched at the foot of the tree and stared at the body on the ground and then stared up at Charlie. The sergeant shouted up to him to get his ass down outta there fast before he lost it, but then he understood and came up after him. He wedged one foot in the fork below where Charlie clung, reached up his hand and held him by the ankle. Then he began to talk to him the way a flight instructor might talk down a rookie pilot panicked by his first solo landing. His voice was hard and low and businesslike.

"Get ahold of yourself there, soldier," he said. "You're coming down now. Just you move this foot when I tell you." He tightened his grip but Charlie's foot didn't move.

He tried again.

"Okay now, here we go. One foot after the other. Just you follow me. You're gonna do fine."

Charlie's foot was solid lead.

The sergeant looked down at the upturned faces on the ground. He looked around him at the other trees. He screwed up his face and thought a moment. Then he changed tactics.

"Move this foot, you sorry asshole!"

Charlie clung to the tree and cried.

"And shut up the racket, damn you! You wanna get yourself greased? You keep that up, you'll get us all greased. You hear me? You shut that up or fucked if I won't shoot you myself."

He jerked at Charlie's obstinate ankle and cursed him. He told him he was the biggest candyassed cocksucker of all time. He told him if he didn't shut up and move he was going to rip him a new asshole big enough for the dinks to drive a whole damn tank batallion through. He called him hard-on, pantiwaist, gook lover, shit-for-brains, crap bucket, turd eater, sombitch, blistered bastard, fucking Girl Scout, and goddammed fuck-faced miserable yellow-bellied mongrel. He called him son-of-a-whoring-bitch and stupid motherfucking shithole prick. He called him the sorriest bastard ever. He demanded to know where his balls where, whether he had any at all, and how would he like to have them served for breakfast?

He cursed Charlie and cursed him. He became a living catalog of soldier curses. Body parts and orifices, excrement and ejaculant, he had them all inside his head and he devoted himself to informing Charlie of them, injecting new and vicious meaning into words worn meaningless with overuse, making each one personal.

He was profane and obscene and abusive.

He held on to Charlie's ankle and cursed on

and on, effortlessly and without stopping for breath. And he kept his voice hard and low and businesslike.

His words smacked up against Charlie's helmet and beat on his head. They jerked around inside his brain and he began to hate the sergeant for his profanity and his crassness and the way he hung onto his ankle and the way the words came pinging out of his mouth like sniper's bullets.

He stopped crying and listened to the words and loathed the sergeant for his low mind and his foul mouth and his clutching hand and the way he kept his voice hard and low and businesslike.

And then he lost his temper. He snatched his ankle out of the sergeant's grasp and smashed his boot down on his helmet.

"Whoa there, asshole! Not so fast! Hey, shithead!"

It was a race.

The two of them slipped and crashed and cursed their way down the tree like men pursued by demons. Once Charlie's heavy boot crushed the sergeant's fingers against a branch and once he swung a satisfying crunch against the side of his head.

Six feet above the ground the sergeant let go and fell the rest of the way. He sprang up immediately, dancing and clinging to his injured fingers.

Then Charlie was down and flying for his throat.

It took four men to drag him away and hold

him off while the sergeant stood and watched, alternately shaking his fingers and blowing on them. With his other hand he reached down into a pocket on the leg of his fatigues and pulled out a cigarette and a metal lighter.

Charlie quieted, glowering at him.

"Feeling better, son?"

The sergeant stuck the cigarette in his mouth and snapped the lighter. He puffed a cloud of smoke and slid the lighter back into his pocket, narrowing his eyes against the smoke. Then he took the cigarette out of his mouth and turned it round, offering it to Charlie. He grinned. He was experienced at this shit. He knew the place for cursing and the place for kindness. He knew how to save a soldier's life.

Charlie lunged at him but he tripped on the sniper's body and came down hard across it.

All the fight went out of him. He propped himself on his hands and began to cry again. He curled his legs up under him and clung to the dead man's black pajama shirt and cried and cried and shook his head and cried, and everyone stood around and stared.

That was when they decided he'd burned out.

"Go to the beach," they said. "Relax. Get your shit back together. And haul your ass back on up here in one week. You're being reassigned."

HOW MINH WAS GONE

So Charlie went to the beach. For three days he lay on the sand at the water's edge and stared into space and gave up his body to the rhythm of the waves. He looked dead and his mind was numb.

On the fourth day in the mid-morning he opened his eyes and saw a local fisherwoman on the beach. She wore a straw coned hat and balanced a pair of baskets on her shoulder on a pole. A little boy trudged behind her holding to the edge of a basket.

Then it occurred to Charlie that he had been in Danang for three days and had not been to see Minh and his son. He had lain on the beach for three whole days and not once in all that time had they so much as crossed his mind.

He thought about them now. He thought about his son. He felt forced to make some sort of decision. But what to do?

Charlie ground through his options.

He could simply go on lying on the beach; ignore the whole thing. Minh didn't know how to contact him. He'd made sure of that. Even if she did, she had no proof he'd married her; he had the wedding certificate tucked into the bottom of his duffle. Yes, ignoring the whole thing would certainly be the easiest way out. It might be the kindest too, come to think of it. He had been a long time out in the jungle without seeing Minh and by now she had more than likely given up on him and gone on with her life. Her mother might even have conned some other unwary American into marrying her. Very likely had. In that case, he shouldn't go. He'd screw things up; run into sucker number two. Might even walk in on him banging Minh on the floor. That would be a bad scene all around.

Charlie nodded to himself. It was decided. He wouldn't go. He relaxed against the sand and closed his eyes.

But his mind wouldn't leave well enough alone. What if there was no second sucker? What if Minh's father had abandoned her? What if her mother had died? What if she had no way to feed herself? What if the child was sick? What if they needed help? He had an obligation. He must go.

But what if her father had drowned the child? He'd threatened it and he was the type to do it. Would he have an obligation then?

But maybe her father had calmed down. He very likely had by now. After all, the kid looked just like Minh. He didn't look American at all. Likely he'd got used to having the kid about the place. Probably looked at him as a grandson by now, loved him even. These Vietnamese had such a thing about their kids. Sure, by now he was bound to be kitchey-cooing or whatever these people did, and taking him around and bragging about him to his friends.

"Look, here's my grandson. Look how big he is, how smart, how cute."

It wouldn't be right to come between the boy and his grandfather; break up a happy family.

No, said Charlie to himself, he shouldn't go.

But maybe they weren't so happy after all. They'd be poor still, wouldn't they? And now they had another mouth to feed. They needed money for that. Where would they get it?

This line of reasoning seemed promising and Charlie applied his mind to it. What if he gave them money? Okay, what if he did? How much? A grand? Two? Three? God, fifty bucks was a fortune to these people. It would be a mistake to give them so much they thought they were rich and hooped it off. It had to be enough but not too much.

He settled on two thousand dollars. He could arrange for that much here. He could pick a time when Minh's father wasn't likely to be around and take it to her. He had an obligation. That's what he should do.

Or should he?

Late in the afternoon a wind sprang up. It lifted the top layer off the sand, swept it down the beach and flung it in a stinging spray against Charlie's sunburned chest. He opened his eyes and came up out of

the water to his hotel. There, he stripped and show-
ered, cleaned his teeth and put some lotion on his
sunburn. He dressed himself and went off to arrange
for the money.

While he was doing it he discovered that
Minh's neighborhood had been declared off limits so
he didn't go to see her right away. It was almost
evening and the military police would be on the
prowl. He would be stopped, for sure. Anyway, he
needed to sleep on this.

He was feeling uneasy now. Would Minh think
he was trying to buy her off? He would be, wouldn't
he? No, not really. He had an obligation to the child.
If he were back home he'd owe its mother child
support. This was no different. He'd just be paying it
up front. Two grand would be enough. It was a
fortune here. It was enough.

He tossed and turned all night. A hundred
times he decided not to do it; he wouldn't go. A
hundred times he changed his mind; two grand would
be the way to go.

The rest of the night he played out confused
half-dreamed scenarios. Once he dreamed he was
back home with Pauline. They were eating dinner in
a restaurant, an expensive one with waiters in bow
ties and starched white napkins folded on their arms.
He wore a pin-striped, three-piece suit and Pauline
wore a pale dress of a shimmery material. It had folds
across the front and fell away so that he could see the

rise of her breasts at the neck. She looked at him across the table and smiled and sipped her wine. She looked at her watch as if to tell him it would soon be time to go.

He was startled at the clearness of this dream and woke telling himself God I could have stayed at home and been a lawyer and been rich and respectable and taken Pauline out to fancy dinners.

He wondered where they had been going, all dressed up like that. To a party? A reception? A show? Maybe a fundraiser; he looked as though he could afford it these days. For sure it would be somewhere where there wouldn't be guns or fire or loud sudden noises.

He closed his eyes. If he could just get back into that dream it would be real. None of this would have happened. It could have been that way. He'd been a fool, a fool.

It was almost morning and he couldn't sleep again so he left his room and went down onto the beach. He had the envelope with the two thousand dollars in his pocket. He hadn't changed it to piasters; it would have been too much to carry.

He walked along the sand, watching the sun come up golden as a ripe mango over the ocean. It was going to be a good day, clear and warm and hot later. Already the beach was littered with the bodies of other soldiers lying at the water's edge and looking dead the way he had the last four days. They didn't look like fighters.

He hoped he wouldn't run into anyone he knew and have to hand out explanations of why he wouldn't join them to do this or that and before long it began to worry him, so he left the beach and wandered off through the streets in the direction of Minh's house.

It was quite far to walk. He could have hailed a taxi but then he would have got there too fast. He needed to work up to this slowly.

He kept an eye out for the military police and told himself he wasn't hoping to be caught.

He was hungry and looked for something good to eat as he went by the street carts and the stores with their sliding metal concertina doors pulled open at the front. He bought a bowl of *pho* and a rice cake from one of the carts and ate it as he walked.

The streets were already busy and filling rapidly with bicycles and motorbikes and buzzing little pedicabs. The sidewalk vendors were setting out their wares. They had yellow mangoes piled on carts and thonged sandals made of rubber piled on the ground beside them, each pair sealed in plastic. Dried fish hung in rows from storefront rafters next to clusters of dried shark's eggs or maybe it was seaweed. And of course there was the panoply of goods filched from Uncle Sam: canned food, watches, jewelry, notebooks, pens and pencils, underwear, makeup, KY jelly, patent medicines, saucepans, black marble saki sets and ornate Chinese vases with pink and gold chrysanthemums painted on them, little imitation bonsai trees and smiling soapstone Bhuddas.

There was no attempt to hide where all these things had come from. Most of them still had stickers showing prices in American dollars.

Charlie examined all this as he went along. It kept his mind off how to handle things at Minh's house. The day had not yet become too hot and he found he was enjoying himself. Things would work out when he got there. No need to worry. He whistled softly to himself under his breath and only hesitated a moment at the corner of Minh's street. He turned it, walking purposefully.

Everything was just the same as always. The sidewalk vendors watched him passing and commented amongst themselves. Old men on their haunches smoked and gossiped in a circle, keeping off the sun with big black broken-spoked umbrellas. Women wearing straws hats on their heads and straw baskets on their arms squeezed at the food laid out along the street and argued over prices.

The little boy in the torn undershirt held out his hand.

"Hi, Joe," he said, expecting nothing.

He had grown taller and wore new bright red pants of some slick fabric that looked like swimming trunks made for a bigger child. His skinny knees stuck out beneath like chicken bones.

Charlie shook his head as he always had and then he changed his mind. He reached into a pocket and gave the child a coin.

It bought him a disciple. The little boy attached himself to Charlie's shadow and followed him off down the road with the coin clutched in his fist. At Minh's door, Charlie noticed him behind. He shooed him with his hands but the child was faithful. He just stood there, clutching the coin and watching.

Minh's door was ajar and there was a rattling going on inside; her mother working at her old black sewing machine.

Charlie felt uncomfortable, as though the whole street were watching him antagonistically. He looked around but it was only the vendors watching as they always did, and his small disciple. It was imagination.

The sun grew hotter as he stood there hesitating. It battered his head. The scene around him shifted subtly. Each object was the same and yet the whole was different. The noises of the street came to him from a distance and he seemed to watch it through a window or an aperture in the wall of another world. It was a foreign world he saw, peopled by foreigners with foreign speech and foreign ways. He didn't belong there. He shouldn't have come.

The rattling of the sewing machine drew him back. He raised his hand to knock but then he couldn't do it. He turned to go but his disciple barred the way, standing with feet apart and mouth ajar, watching devotedly.

Charlie drew a breath, swung back towards the door and knocked, all in a single motion.

The sewing machine rattled on.

He pushed the door, stepped through and looked for Minh but there was no-one there; just a stout peasant woman in a room treadling an ancient sewing machine. The room was poor and dreary and unutterably foreign.

He watched the woman as she sewed. She was intent on a piece of black fabric that she held with one hand on each side of the needle and coaxed through. She watched the path of the needle closely while she pumped and pumped the treadle. The machine shook and rattled and the needle clicked obediently up and down.

Charlie coughed but no response. He moved closer, going to the front of the machine where she would surely see him. He coughed again softly, not wanting to startle her. She must have noticed him by now.

But Minh's mother was in no hurry. She finished the seam to the very edge before she lifted her head, keeping her hand on the wheel of the machine in case her foot should, unintended, press down on the treadle and set the needle moving. Her face turned in his direction but blankness sat on her features and her eyes looked through him at the wall behind. She sighed.

Charlie moved the muscles of his face to make a smile but they seemed to have lost connection with the corners of his mouth. He struggled with his face.

"Hi." It was a whisper.

He cleared his throat and tried again.

"Hi."

The peasant woman had a yellow discoloration on one side of her face close to the eye, a half-healed bruise. She turned back to her work, twitching the fabric around and trundling down another seam. When it was done, she took her foot off the treadle, raised the needle with a little snapping sound, and broke the thread. Meticulously she pulled one thread through the fabric to join its mate on the other side. She tied them together and snipped off the trailing thread with a tiny pair of scissors. She set the garment aside and turned her bruised face towards Charlie again. There was no sign of recognition, no curiosity.

"I've been away, out in the jungle. It's been a while, I know it's been a while, too long...Is Minh around? I've come to see her. Where's the boy? He must have grown."

The stout peasant didn't speak although her eyes were focussed on him now. He smiled at them uneasily.

"I've brought her something...just a...well,

some money actually. I thought it might help with the boy...with Charlie. I, well, you might..."

He stopped, intimidated by her gaze. It was as though she'd never known him. She looked at him as though he were a stranger, an intruder in her home. He looked nervously towards the door but there was no-one there.

"I'm real sorry to have missed her. I'd like to wait till she gets back but I don't have the time. I have to get back to base, you see. I shouldn't be here at all really. Would you give this to her for me?" He drew the envelope out of his pocket and held it out but she ignored it so he set it down by the sewing machine.

"It's for you both...things you might need...the boy..."

There was a flicker in the woman's eyes and Charlie had a sudden panicked feeling that something had happened to Minh. Her father? Had he done something to her? Or to the child? Had her father drowned it after all?

The yellow bruise on the woman's face seemed to accuse him. Where had she got such a bruise? Her husband had beaten her surely. Had it been on account of him? Had he brought violence to this family? But how could that be? He had loved them. He searched inside his heart for the love to prove it to himself but there was only hollowness inside.

Where had it gone, the love?

He stared stupidly at the stout woman until

he couldn't bear the yellow accusation of her face any more and then he turned his head away and went towards the door.

"Well, I'll be off," he said without looking back, a stupid thing to say.

As he stepped outside, he heard the woman's stool scrape back and tip over with a crack on the cement floor. He turned and she was in the doorway reaching out towards him with the envelope of money. Her face was angry now but still she didn't meet his eye.

For a moment Charlie didn't recognize this woman who was Minh's mother at all. He'd given the money to the wrong person. No wonder she had looked at him so strangely.

She shouted something angry in Vietnamese and flung the envelope at him. It smacked against his chest and the money flew out and sprayed around his feet. The woman vanished back inside the house, slamming the door so hard that the front wall of the shoddy structure shook and bits of plaster fell down out of the eaves.

Charlie stood there staring. He was astonished. This woman was as proud as an American.

His small disciple, who had been waiting patiently outside the door all this time, now fell down onto his haunches and, scuttling around like a spider, scooped up all the money in the space of seconds. He sprang to his feet with it clutched against his chest and would have run but Charlie was too quick. He reached down and grabbed him by the shoulder.

"Hold it, kid! Hold it right there!"

He crouched before the boy, a hand on each shoulder, holding tight. The boy met his gaze defiantly and tightened his grip on the money.

Charlie looked at him standing there in his baggy red pants with the prize of his life clutched to his chest and his anger vanished in a sudden recklessness. Well, damn the woman! If she didn't want it, he'd give it to someone who did.

"Do you understand any English besides hi Joe?"

The boy stared defiantly.

Still holding him by one shoulder, Charlie touched a finger to the clutching fists. The boy flinched back and tensed all over.

"You want it, kid? It's yours. Don't spend it all in one place."

The boy twisted suddenly, jerked his shoulder out of Charlie's grasp and ran like a rabbit down the street, darting in and out of legs and street carts with his baggy red pants flapping about his knees.

"Hey, kid!"

The kid had vanished.

Charlie ran his hand across his hair and shrugged.

"Well, what the hell."

He went drinking that night and got very drunk. A bar girl came and sat on his knee and stroked his face but he said he was a married man and interested only in whisky. He tried to think about Minh and her child but he could only remember a stout peasant woman with a bruised accusing face and a grubby urchin with red baggy pants and two thousand Yankee dollars clutched in his fists.

He drank until he calculated he would pass out on the next shot and then he bought the rest of the bottle from the barman, went back to his hotel and finished off the job.

That was his fifth day of leave.

The sixth day he spent propped against the head of his bed telling himself that drinking all night was a very bad thing to do.

Late in the afternoon, when the ocean had become flat and reflective, he went outside wearing dark glasses and holding his head straight and steady on his neck. He went down into the water until it was high on his thighs and sat down carefully with the underside of his chin just touching the surface. Neither he nor the ocean moved at all.

When it was dark the ocean woke from its evening meditation and rocked him back and forth unpleasantly. He left it then and sat down at its edge with his knees bent. He watched the moon in the sky and the water making its advance towards him up the sand, shuffling his body backwards when it got too close.

When the tide was fully in he stood up and walked back to his hotel where he went to bed and slept all night without dreaming.

On the seventh day of his leave he woke early, feeling strong, and ate a good breakfast of bacon and eggs with toast and grape jelly and thick dark coffee. Then he cleaned his teeth and combed his hair. He took his newly cleaned and pressed fatigues out of the closet and his newly polished boots from beside the bed and put them on. After that he went out to the balcony overlooking the beach and sat down to write a letter to Pauline.

It wasn't special, just a soldier's letter to his wife. He told her that the weather was hot generally but cold out in the jungle early in the morning. He told her he was well and hoped she was the same and that he looked forward very much to coming home. He said the war was going well, which he didn't know but presumed to be the case, and that it would be over soon he'd heard, although he hadn't, but it was the sort of thing a soldier should say to his wife.

He enjoyed writing the letter because it was plain and straightforward and there was nothing sudden or perplexing in it and when he read it over it gave him a fine feeling of stolid worthiness. He calculated in his head how long it would take for Pauline to get it and how long it would be for him to get a letter back from her. He knew he could rely on her to answer right away so he added no time for her to get around to it.

When that was done he mailed the letter, packed his duffle, and hauled his ass on back as he had been ordered.

Seamless blue sky rushed past the helicopter's door and down below ten thousand shades of green ran all together. Charlie watched the door gunner watching it all. That was his job: watch and watch and shoot and shoot, and when there was nothing to see, shoot anyway. It was a very loud job he had. Charlie had forgotten how loud it was to be a soldier. Watching the door gunner doing his job reminded him.

He didn't think about Danang.

Halfway back to base it occurred to him that he was relieved about the way things had turned out there. He looked at the head of the door gunner silhouetted against the sky and listened to the thump, thump, thumping of the blades above his head; and for the rest of the trip he thought about nothing at all.

HOW HE HEARD THE HELICOPTER

He could hear it still, the helicopter. It hummed and buzzed just above the tree line. He couldn't see it yet because it was dark but it was there, coming towards him. When it got close it would turn on its spotlight and he would run out of the darkness into its circle of brightness.

A wave of exuberance shuddered through him. He would run out into the spotlight and shout and wave and jump. And there would be faces in the doorway of the helicopter, smiling faces, and arms waving back at him, and voices calling, calling down to him out of the sky. Coming to take him back to safety, back to where he wouldn't itch so. He would have a bath. He would shave. He would go to the hospital and have his chigger bites fixed. Then he'd go back to the platoon, tramp around with them looking for a safe place to spend the day, trade some jokes, listen to one of Lou's letters.

Ah, but Lou was dead now, wasn't he? They all were.

He moved restlessly, waiting for the helicopter. He could hear it in the tunnel now. It was coming fast, straight at him.

He sat up with a jerk, his hands out in the

darkness protecting his face, flailing about blindly.

Keep it off me. Keep it off me.

It was silent now and he desperately rubbed his hands over his face and neck, his arms, his ankles. Don't let it land. Don't let it bite. It started up again and he tracked its flight, listening carefully, holding out his hands to trap it, slapping the palms sharply together, slapping his face, his legs, his arms.

Silence again. Listen. There it is. Slap. No there. Slap. There, there.

Silence. Had he got it? Was it squashed between his hands? He felt the palms carefully. Nothing. Was he wearing it on his face, squashed flat, wearing it like a scar, like a blind man with odd socks? He rubbed his face carefully all over. Then his neck.

Every part of exposed flesh he rubbed down, cleaning off the corpse, cleaning off Lou's corpse, cleaning off the blood, someone's brains, the letters from Lou's wife, the memory of it all.

HOW LT WAS A PEACEFUL MAN

They reassigned him to a platoon undersized enough to be no bigger than a squad where all the men had something they didn't speak about, thin men with thin eyes; and when Charlie had been with them a while he wondered if perhaps the nature of this platoon were known, if perhaps the military had a heart, because all these men were like him: beyond killing.

LT was in charge of the platoon and he was a man with a single luminous goal: to keep his men alive.

"I'm a peaceful man," he would sigh. "A peaceful man."

But LT wasn't a pacifist. He had no political position, no broad view of the war, no opinions. He just had his goal. It hung in front of him like a guiding star and he kept his men alive. If he had to kill the enemy, so be it. He would be cold and decisive, killing them first. But he didn't engage intentionally, ever. He made his own war, dreaming up elaborate plans for how to avoid contact.

"My men don't die," he told Charlie the day he joined them. "I'm here to keep my men alive." It wasn't braggadocio, just a statement of fact.

His men thought he was lucky. They stuck close to him as though his luck would rub off on them. And it did seem to. He hadn't lost one so far.

LT had rules. No coming out drunk was one, but top of his list was no drugs.

"That stuff messes up your head," he said. "That's the way to end up dead. No point in being dead."

His little band of men agreed with him. They had no wish to die either, so they sought out safe places and made up tales of conquest and manufactured numbers for the body count; or they just saw nothing at all, which wasn't so unusual. If they were pushed to make contact, they made sure they all sang from the same hymn book, and if they made contact by accident, they fought to preserve each other. They were a tight group, watching out for each other. For them the war was dull and hot and fearful.

At first Charlie found a guilty relief in this way of operating. He had no choice, really, but to go along with it. He had no desire to die, and no longer any stake in killing.

But then there was the fear.

When he became a soldier, fear became his friend, his most faithful companion. Its sudden peaking rushes of adrenaline sharpened his mind and propelled him into action. It was action that controlled the fear.

Now fear became his enemy, a humming low-level thing that fed on itself and grew into a looming darkness that hung inside his head and blackened his imagination. It seemed to him better to stand and fight. Fighting was bad, but fear was worse.

He never spoke these thoughts. Instead, he let himself become part of the platoon as it crept and hid with the specter of death following, slipping in and out between the towering strangled trees, lurking amongst the great winged roots that rose suddenly out of the ground like sailing ships, peering at them from the mist, filling the jungle with its insistent drip dripping, like blood from a wound.

After a skirmish, the tension would ease for a while and the face of death would recede. And then the long, heavy days would run into each other, one on one on one, and the tension would build again while LT planned his elaborate avoidance maneuvers; and the fear would come back with it.

It was the fear that finally got Wiley Rattley and punched a hole in LT's perfect score.

Wiley Rattley was a panic-stricken boy from West Virginia, a farmhand. He was tall and long-jointed, and he had a phenomenal beard. He shaved, as they all did, peering into a little mirror propped in the cleft of a tree and scraping diligently. But no sooner done, it seemed, than the stubble sprang up again. It caught the heat and irritation in the air and he complained and scratched at it constantly, pushing his face this way and that with the backs of his knuckles.

But although he was tall and big of beard, Wiley Rattley was just a boy, a tall boy, frightened as a man.

He showed his fear like the boy he was, like a child: in his hands, the way they beat at his chin, and in his body, the way he walked with his head pulled back on his neck and met no-one's eye and licked his lips until they were raw and jerked off in the night for comfort.

On his helmet he had written the months of his tour. The last one was March. It was August now. He'd been in LT's platoon five months.

"What happened to the rest of your months?" Charlie asked one day.

Wiley laughed a high-toned, girlish laugh. "There ain't no more," he said. "I'm daid. The gooks cain't get me now."

"How much time you got?"

He looked at Charlie slyly. "I got forever, man. Forever. Damn gooks cain't get me now."

He never had a chance really. He fought as well as any and never ran. But it was fear that got him in the end, the enemy inside. He came to war with it and fought with it day after day until it got him.

He didn't die a coward and he didn't die a hero. His death was just an ordinary soldier's death. An interchange of fire across a ridge and when it was done Wiley was dead, shot cleanly through the eye. A painless death. And although it was the bullet that finished him off, it was the fear that had eaten away his insides. He would have died of it anyway. The bullet just put him out of his misery.

When he was gone and the helicopter carrying his body had vanished, sobbing its way off across the treetops, LT did not speak. He stared after the sound, standing with his foot on a rock, his helmet dangling from one hand and the other hanging limp and heavy at his side. He looked pulled down, as though gravity had intensified in his small spot of earth.

He said nothing for the longest time and they all stood around and watched him fearfully.

At last it was Dan who spoke. He was a medic and he had a gentle way with him. He laid his hand on LT's shoulder.

"It's the war."

LT sighed a long, deep sigh. He twisted his head and moved his shoulders as though his neck hurt.

"Damn the war," he said.

LT took Wiley's death personally. It upset him a lot.

"My men don't die," he would say, as if in disbelief. "I'm here to see to it."

For weeks he sat apart, brooding in silence. Sometimes he would punch the ground and say, "We should have waited till daylight," or, "We should have cut around to the west."

He took to walking with his flak jacket open, as if tempting fate to punish him for failing Wiley. He developed nosebleeds and let the blood run down onto his chest. Sometimes he would stumble when he walked, his legs moving in spastic jerks. He would drink and drink until his bladder couldn't hold it any more and then he would unzip his pants and stand watching the bright yellow pee arc through the air, and complain that he was thirsty. On each side of his head a ragged strip of gray appeared and his eyes became opaque. He turned them inward and smiled a dreamy smile.

His men watched him furtively from the corners of their eyes and never asked the question on their minds: has LT lost his luck? They just watched him and didn't get too close. They began to look for omens and give each other things they said were lucky: a pebble with a glowing stripe, a crucifix, a blossom from a dogwood tree sent in the mail. They moved more warily than before and forgot to sleep. Their eyes grew red with weariness and they walked like zombies through the steaming heat.

There came a day, though, when LT returned from wherever he had been and they forgot about their trinkets. The pebble was tossed at a bird. The crucifix fell unnoticed into the mud and was trampled underfoot. The dogwood blossom turned to crumbs in someone's pocket and was shaken out onto the ground. The platoon came back to life.

The fear was with them still but they knew how to deal with it now that LT was back. They slipped ahead of it and hid till it had passed.

And when it closed around them in the night they held it off with jokes and banter, tales of women, beer and childhood and, from time to time, with Lou's letters from his wife.

HOW LOU WOULD READ HIS LETTERS

Lou's wife was Tammy and she wrote him wild, sexy, irregular letters.

Louie, she would write, *Louie, my love, my joy, my pride, my all...*

And Lou would read it out aloud to them all, balancing the letter on his knee, shining his penlight slowly down the page, shielding it with his hand, as though to keep Tammy's passionate outpourings from jumping off it. Because Tammy was passionate.

Lying in bed last night, she wrote, *I thought about your big cock. Remember how we used to...*

And Lou would read it all out to them, his little penlight making its way along each line and down to the next.

When you get back, Tammy wrote, *I'm going to suck...*

And Lou read it all out in his thick level voice, as though he were reading Proust or the Bible.

Lou wasn't shy about what his wife wanted to do with his body. Down the page his penlight would go, his wife's plump white limbs thrashing and writhing in the watching darkness, the sloppy sounds of her sucking rippling off into the listening silence.

And when he had read every word start to

finish and gone back and read the best bits over again, to a chorus of, "Read the bit about," and groans, he would fold up the letter into a neat little packet. Then he'd fumble around inside the pocket of his fatigues and bring out the rest of them, clamped together with the two rubber bands, a red one across, a green one down.

Holding his penlight between his teeth he would snap off the rubber bands, setting them carefully side by side on his knee. He would add the latest letter to the top of the pile, tap them together on his knee to get them straight, and snap the rubber bands back on, the red one first, then the green one, with a triumphant ping.

"That's all for now folks!" he would say, and flick off the penlight.

They'd huddle down for the night then and when they slept they'd dream of Tammy's luscious body and her juicy mouth sucking, sucking. And Charlie, on watch, would see her white limbs writhing in the haunted darkness and hear the smack of her lips.

And then he would press his ear to the ground and imagine he heard the hum of a city down there. And he would picture it in the darkness: a great city with highways and cars humming and houses in rows, with fences and children playing and people coming and going and sidewalks with trees and a tall man walking his dog; and Tammy and Lou inside one of the houses making mad, passionate love.

But there wasn't a city down there, just a black hole in the ground, with him sitting in it like a blind animal in a cage, and all the rest dead.

It was Tammy's fault. She had got them all killed. All but him, though he may as well have been dead because here he was, in this hole in the ground where he would probably die with her letters in his pocket, her damnable letters.

Yes, Tammy had killed them all, sure as shooting: LT and Dan and Sal and Mack the Knife and Harold T. Booker. All of them.

HOW SAL LIKED HAROLD T. BOOKER

Harold T. Booker was Wiley Rattley's replacement. He was the biggest, blackest man in the whole world.

That's what Sal said. "The biggest, blackest man that ever walked the earth," he said.

At first it looked as though Harold T. would have some trouble fitting in. He rolled into camp with a swagger.

"What all's this?" he demanded. "Some sorta honky outfit? Where's all the brothers?"

Sal objected. "Don't call me honky," he said. "I'm pure P.R. What's your credentials?"

Harold T. Booker looked at him. "I'm mean," he said. "That's my credentials. Where you got the brothers hid?"

Mack was picking at his toes with a knife. He looked up, balancing the knife by the blade. "No brothers here," he said. "We gave 'em all to Charlie."

LT intervened. "Okay," he said. "Okay."

He introduced himself. "And this is Dan, and Mack and Sal and Lou. That's all we've got right now except for that one over there taking a leak. Hey, Charlie! This is Harold T."

Charlie came over and stuck out a hand. "Hi. I'm Charlie."

"You jerkin' me?"

Charlie scratched his head and shrugged.

Mack grinned. "He ate the brothers, Harold T. You watch yourself with Charlie."

Harold T's face turned truculent and LT tensed to intervene again, but Sal broke in. "You play football, Harold T? Sure looks like. What position you play? Offensive tackle? Defensive end? Looks like you would, big dude like you."

The tension came off. Harold T. Booker laughed. "Played once," he said. "But now I'm just a big black brother, a ba-ad dude." He bellied up to Charlie and stuck his face up close. "You wanna eat me, honky Charles?"

Charlie just grinned and wandered off. He squatted down beside Mack and watched him picking at his toes with the knife.

Before long Harold T. came and squatted with them and began to talk. He was a talker. Charlie smiled and ducked his head, a listener. The others edged closer. Harold T. was the sort of man who invited an audience.

He came from Washington, D.C. "Off of H Street, behind your nation's Capitol, that's where I'm from, man," he told them. "I'm the big bad spade from off of H Street."

Charlie was from D.C. too.

"Where 'bouts you from in D.C.?" asked Harold T. Booker. "You sure nuff ain't from off of H

Street." He rolled his eyes and laughed, a big man's laugh, deep down and low. "Where you from, white boy?"

Charlie was from Georgetown.

"Well, I just mighta guessed it," said Harold T. Booker. "White boy like you, lookin' down his white boy's nose and sayin' all his words correct." He flicked a piece of grass. "We all equal now though, ain't we, white boy? Out here we equals. You watch my black ass, I watch your white one. We both of us watch out for little yellow asses." He fell into a philosophical mood. "The world is full of colored ass."

"The only colored ass I want to see round here," said LT, "is red, white and blue."

Harold T. Booker laughed. "You right, man," he said. "You very right. That ass out there ain't red, white and blue, shoot it, it's a gook."

Harold T. had a bad attitude towards Charlie. It wasn't anything that happened or anything that Charlie did. And it wasn't intense enough for hatred or even what might be called dislike. He called him white boy and honky Charles sometimes but most of the time he just had a bad attitude. Sometimes he forgot and was expansive and other times he remembered and wasn't.

Charlie didn't pay too much attention to it. It didn't signify enough to be a danger to the platoon, although anything like that could start to be any time at all. So it was a relief when Harold T. got over it.

It was the Johnson's baby powder that did it.

Harold T. had not been with the platoon for very long when he developed trouble in his crotch. He said nothing about it, in fact he stopped saying much about anything at all. He developed an odd stare.

"What's up with you?" said Sal. "Something wrong? Your tongue fall out?"

"Shut up, turkey."

"Say what?"

"Shut up. I said shut up."

"Okay, okay."

Harold T. developed an odd walk too. He moved his legs carefully and held them wide apart. When he wasn't walking he pulled constantly at the crotch of his fatigues, looking furtive, like a kindergartner who's peed his pants.

One day Sal asked again.

"Now look here, bro. I just marched twenty miles behind your stinkin' ass and you got something wrong. You better tell afore you die of it. Come on Harold T, don't be an asshole." He grinned, cajoling. "Tell your Uncle Sal."

Harold T. gave in. "I got the clap I think. M'balls are falling off."

"Damn fool."

They had found themselves a nice hilltop that

promised nothing in the way of action and were digging in.

Sal called across to Dan. "Harold T. here's got the clap."

"Don't have to shout, turkey," said Harold T.

"Only us here. Gooks don't give a damn about your balls anyways, 'cept to blow them off."

Dan came up. "What?"

"Our man's got clap."

Dan wrinkled his nose. "I don't do clap. You need a shot. Ought to keep your balls out of chicken houses, Harold T."

"Aw, come on Dan. Take a look at the man's balls, will ya?"

"Well then, drop 'em."

The others had finished digging in now and came to see.

"Get outa here! I ain't showing m'balls to the world. Go watch out for dinks."

Mack and Lou went off to stand guard. Sal stayed and Dan spread out a poncho on the ground. "Get down on here so I can see."

LT and Charlie squatted on their packs and watched the trees. Harold T. turned his back to them, dropped his pants and sat on the poncho with his knees spread.

Sal flapped at the flies to keep them off while Dan inspected his balls.

"Not clap."

"Then what?"

"Crotchrot."

"Ah, shit! What you got?"

Dan poked through his bag. "Here, this'll hold you till we get back to base. You should have paid attention, you dumb shit. It's climbing on your dick."

"Don't call me dumb shit."

"You hear what I said? You shoulda had this seen to."

"Okay! I'm sorry, sorry! Goddamm! You're hurting."

"Hold still. How can I do this when your balls are flying about?"

"Sorry! I said sorry!"

"It goes up inside your dick you'll be sorry."

"What you doing down there, anyways?"

"He's paintin' your balls red, bro," said Sal.

Harold T. twisted down to see.

"Hey, lookit that!"

Dan finished painting.

"What you need is to keep your crotch dry. It's sweating does it."

"Cain't help it. Fuckin' weather makes a mother sweat like a pig. I gone through more under-shorts than all my life out here. Goddammed things just fall apart."

Sal laughed. "You're hot stuff."

Dan was thinking. "You need powder." He raised his voice. "Anyone got powder?"

Charlie carried Johnson's baby powder in his pack. It was part of his legacy of advice from Dougherty. He got up off his pack and dug around inside it.

"Here." He took it over, twisting the lid.

"You keep that white boy off me," Harold said.

Charlie laughed. "Powder your own balls," he said, tossing Harold T. the can. He went back to squat on his pack.

So Harold T. sprayed powder on his balls while Sal crouched beside him, giving advice.

"Here, lift 'em higher. Higher, bro. You missed a bit. Do right up your dick so it don't travel. There, that's good. Hey, Harold T., guess what?"

"What?" He tossed the powder back to Charlie.

"You got pink balls."

Harold T. twisted for another look. "Well, I'll be damned! Look what you done to me," he called to Charlie. "I got pink balls, just like yours."

Charlie had the baby powder in his hands and was twisting the lid closed. He grinned and stuffed it back into his pack. "I guess we're brothers now," he said.

"You put them balls away, Harold T," Sal said. "You leave 'em hangin' out, dinks are goin' to blow 'em off you."

Harold T. got up off the poncho and hitched up his pants. He pulled at the zipper gingerly, standing with his legs apart and his knees bent. Then he snapped his belt buckle closed and slowly straightened his knees. He grinned at Charlie. "I guess we are," he said. He had white hand prints in his crotch.

It was after that Harold T. began to develop a better attitude to Charlie. He stopped calling him white boy and honky Charles and the whole platoon moved a little tighter.

Sal, on the other hand, never had a problem with Harold T. He liked him from the start. He liked him because he was a big man. Sal liked big men. He liked football players. He talked about heights and weights all the time.

"Six foot four and two eighty," he would say, and hiss between his teeth admiringly. "How 'bout that?"

Sal wasn't a small man himself, not really, five nine or so, not small. But he loved size. He never got letters from home, not real ones, just cover letters from his mother.

Here you are, she would write. *The latest.* She sent him the sports pages of the New York Times, a week's worth at a time with a cover letter. Not that Sal had anything against the Stars and Stripes. He read that too but when it came to sports reporting, a little paper like that just wasn't enough for him. He wanted the real thing.

In volume Sal got more mail than any of them

but it was all newspaper with little short cover letters. Not even letters really, just notes. *Here you are,* they'd say, *the latest.*

Once she wrote, *Your dad's been sick and off work but he's back now.* And another time she wrote, *They say on the T.V. there's been a moratorium about the war but I think it's just another demonstration.* Mostly she just wrote, *Here you are, the latest.*

And Sal would read the latest start to finish and tell about the heights and weights with shining eyes.

He left them behind when he'd read them, just left them where they lay when he'd done. All up and down the jungle he left them, the sports pages of the New York Times, littering Vietnam with the heights and weights of big men.

One day he rigged a sunshield out of Bubba Smith. He'd finished reading and he took a couple of the double pages and set them on his head.

"Whatcha doin', fool?" from Harold T.

Sal didn't answer. He held his head carefully so the newspaper wouldn't fall off and clamped his helmet over it. It stuck out behind his neck like a pair of wings.

"What, you gonna fly?"

"It's for the sun, smartass, to keep it off m'neck."

Charlie walked behind Sal that day and watched the paper flapping up and down on Sal's neck. On the left there was a picture of someone leaping through the air, caught mid-flight in a tackle. Charlie peered closer. He could see his number and the insignia on his helmet. Baltimore Colts, number 78. Bubba Smith. Another of America's big black men. He'd seen him play once when he was with Michigan State. It was a good game. Bubba was the hero. When he came out onto the field the crowd chanted, "Kill, Bubba! Kill!" They called him Interballistic Bubba. He could fly.

All day Charlie watched Bubba Smith do his flying tackle, sometimes imagining that he really saw him move. They marched through jungle clouded thick with steam and slopped their way through sucking mud up to their knees and all the way Bubba Smith flew at his man. There was a cloud of flies on Sal's back and the flapping paper had them agitated. They kept swarming up a few inches into the air and settling back down.

Then it began to rain.

It didn't start gently and work up. It just fell down without warning in belting sheets and the wind rushed it sideways. Within thirty seconds the sky looked like the rippled surface of the ocean, the flies were gone and Bubba Smith was drowned.

Charlie stared into the blackness and thought about Sal and the trail of sports pages he left behind. He wondered if Victor Charlie ever picked them up and read them. Six four and two eighty, he'd read, the little five nothing, ninety pound man.

Of course, he wouldn't believe it. No-one could be that big, not even Americans. It was all just propaganda, left around to frighten them with heights and weights of the enemy, like Gulliver stomping up and down in Lilliput.

But they'd got him, hadn't they, the Lilliputians? Those little fellows had got him. So where's your height and weight now, Gulliver?

He fell to thinking about the Lilliputians he called Man One and Man Two. Man One was the smaller, very light and delicate in his bones, like Minh. Ah, Minh. He could think about her now as if she'd never happened.

He wondered where Man One had learned his bit of English. Had he once lived somewhere else? Or had he lived his life entirely in the dark, creeping out at nightfall, vanishing at dawn? Did he go home to some *ville* to sleep or did he sleep in tunnels? Was he a creature of the jungle?

Charlie remembered the haunted nights he'd spent sitting cross-legged and still as death, hidden in his poncho, his finger on the trigger, imagining he saw the little people in the dark. They were magic little people. Here they were. No, there they were. Up there. Down there. No, no-one there at all.

They left behind them pieces of themselves:

warm ashes, footprints sometimes, broken twigs, an empty bunker backed into a hill. And always they were all around and never there, like fairies, goblins, elves. They vanished like a vapor, reformed like the condensation of an essence called up from another world. They came in dreams and nightmares, stealthy, deadly, slipping from the corners of the eyes.

On more than one occasion Charlie had convinced himself that they were phantoms, nothing real, a figment of imagination. But then he'd smell them out there, evil spirits bringing odors out of hell.

He smelled them now, moving softly in the tunnel. Sweat burst out in a panic on his forehead, in his groin. A candle flickered. He screwed his eyes and opened them. There, they were real. The little people.

"You okay, Chah-ree?"

It was only Man One and Man Two come to do their chores.

"Okay, Chah-ree?"

Man One seemed concerned. Why should he care? He crouched beside him, rolling out his riceball, trickling water into his canteen. They'd brought another jar, a replacement for the one that now seemed always to be on the brink of overflowing. Man One lifted his chin towards the old one and Man Two set down his rifle and went about removing it. He slid it onto a piece of heavy plastic and pulled it carefully towards the tunnel entrance, going backwards and edging it along after him.

Charlie eyed the rifle on the floor. What if he jumped for it? Was there a chance? Man One was screwing on the lid of his canteen, looking down.

Charlie's muscles tightened for the spring.

But then he realized that Man One had stopped his screwing. He'd stopped his breathing too. Charlie felt his eyes upon him. He let his muscles loosen. How had he known? He hadn't moved at all. Could this man hear muscles flex?

Man Two came back and it was over.

Charlie watched them go through their routine. Man One had no shirt on and he watched his body, picking out what seemed to be a round, clean scar low on his chest. When he turned his back, there was another, unmistakable even in the dim light, still dark-edged and ragged, snaking from shoulder to waist. Man One wasn't skinny in an awkward way, but thin, so very thin, and slight, a fragile enemy. He looked like Minh.

Ah, Minh. Don't think about her now. Think of Pauline.

He thought about Pauline. A sterling woman that. A woman to be proud of. She was a beauty too and smart and very conscientious. She wrote to him like clockwork, her letters postmarked exactly seven days apart. They could be relied on.

Dear Charlie, Pauline wrote, *Thank you for the*

letter. It's nice to know that you are well.

She wrote, *Dear Charlie, Have finished the first ten pages of my dissertation. It's rather interesting, this stuff.*

He could remember what her letters said exactly because they were all the same. The words were different and the sentences were too but still the letters were the same.

Dear Charlie, they said, *love, Pauline.* They were cool and practical and strong. Cool practical letters from a cool practical woman. They were letters with straight backs. Pauline had a straight back.

Her letters never frightened him or made him cry or wonder. He could rely on them always to be the same.

Dear Charlie, wrote Pauline, so cool and correct, *had another chat with the old fellow next door. Do you remember him? He came to that party we had and was quite perky and complained about the noise next day. Remember? You said he was an ungrateful old wart and so he was.*

Anyway, he has turned out to be very nice and has been quite a friend to me. He is very interested in you and in the war. He reads everything about it in the papers and watches all the news on television although he only sees the pictures because he is deaf.

He complains that the announcers don't speak clearly. He does complain a lot but I think it is because he doesn't like to be old. He would like to be young again and maybe live forever.

Anyway, he asks about you all the time and wants to know if you are seeing any action. He had a brother in the First World War and tells me all about him.

He calls the First World War the Big One as though no other war could match it...

Charlie remembered the old man. Of course he did. He turned up at their party and drank without stopping, talking all the time and pinching women, until he was so drunk he couldn't get out of his chair. They were afraid he would die, drinking so much at his age. But he didn't. He lived to complain about the noise. And they had asked him in the first place so he wouldn't. He was an ungrateful wart.

Charlie had a vision of Pauline sitting upright in the front parlor of this old fossil's house having a chat.

"Oh, yes," she said. "Lovely weather indeed. What's that you say? How is Charlie? Oh, Charlie's very well, thank you. Doing his bit." And she laughed, not letting on about anything.

Pauline never let on about anything not even in her letters. Especially not there.

Dear Charlie, said her letters, *love, Pauline.*

Did she still write to him? Where were her letters then? Did they send them back or burn them? Or were they in a pile in someone's office? Some dead letter office. Letters for dead people. Stop that. No point in being morbid.

Of course she wouldn't write. Not now. By now they would have told her. They would have sent her a letter.

Sorry to inform you, it would say, *your husband Charlie Lucas is missing.* Missing presumed dead. He's dead, Mrs. Lucas. We're sure he died a hero but we can't confirm it so there won't be any medals. Anyway, he's dead. As a matter of fact, it was the least he could do. He was a soldier after all. If he didn't want to die he would have gotten himself out of the draft, now wouldn't he? He wouldn't have been there in the first place. Only people with a death wish go to Vietnam. So you see, Mrs. Lucas, he got what he asked for. He deserved to die.

Stop it! Stop right there.

"How's Charlie?" asks the fossil when Pauline comes to see him, shouting because he is deaf. "He seen any action lately?"

Pauline sits up very straight. "Oh yes," she says. "He's seen quite a bit. He's missing in it actually."

"Eh? What's that you say?"

"Missing. Charlie's missing."

"You miss him?" He fiddles with his hearing aid, complaining. "I can't hear you properly. Speak clearly. Weren't you ever taught to speak clearly, girlie?"

"I said he's missing," speaking very clearly.

The old boy sucks his teeth and looks knowing. "Said that about my brother. Missing they said
first then killed in action. It's inevitable. He was
blown up. That's what happens to them. They say
missing but really they're blown up. My brother was
blown up." He leers at her. "Blown to bits, just all to
bits. Nothing to bring back home they said. It's inevitable in a war. They die. They always die. They die of
one thing or another."

Ungrateful wart. She is his friend. No need to
talk to her like that.

But Pauline sits up very straight not letting on
about anything. A sterling woman that. A rock. If he
could hold to her he wouldn't drown. She knows it
too. She married him for that. It wasn't pity after all.
It was to give him something strong to hold to so he
wouldn't drown. She is his anchor in a dangerous
sea.

The sea is flat and black and on the surface it
is still but underneath there is a rip. It is fast and very
strong and it never stops. If he lets go it will drown
him but if he holds on tight to Pauline the rip will not
sweep him away. When it drags him out very long
and rushing it will not drown him if he can just fix his
mind very hard on her.

Think about Pauline.

Charlie leans forward and looks over her shoulder.
She is sitting at the desk in her little study carrel in

the basement of the library. She is writing on a yellow pad with pale green lines and talking to herself.

"Ten pages of dissertation," she says. "And now it's time to write to Charlie."

She reaches up and pulls a box of notepaper off the shelf above her head. She writes her dissertation on a yellow lined pad but she writes to him on notepaper. It is white and plain and of the highest quality. It is correct.

Dear Charlie, she writes, and, *love, Pauline.*

A letter to Charlie and ten pages of dissertation. Then another letter to Charlie and then ten more pages of dissertation.

She is doing her dissertation on some Scottish philosopher. What was his name, Paul?

"Hume," she says.

Hume, that was it, David Hume.

"David Hume, the eminent Scottish philosopher," she says, laughing to herself at some private joke. "Odd ideas he had about the world, you know. They don't seem to be connected to reality. Come to think of it, Charlie," and she turns to look, "you don't yourself. Is that really you?"

"Yes, it's me."

"You're rather blurry."

"It's because I'm not connected to reality."

"Oh, I see. In that case I'd better get back to my dissertation."

A practical woman. A rock. She is connected

to reality.
Dear Charlie, love, Pauline.

He thought about reality. He wasn't connected to it now. All he had left of it were Lou's letters from Tammy sitting heavy in his pocket. Her wild hot letters that she wrote and mailed sporadically when she was in the mood. He wished they were Pauline's. Pauline was a rock but Tammy was a millstone around Lou's neck. Around all their necks. She pulled them down and drowned them. She was not a sterling woman.

HOW MACK DREW A PICTURE OF THE WAR

Lou's letters from Tammy were rude and raunchy. They seemed to be directed at them all like a strip-tease act or a visit to the local hooker.

Lou, babe, she would write, *You've got the cutest buns. Did I ever tell you about your buns? So tight and round and hard. I want to lick them, Lou. I want to stick my face up between your cheeks and tickle that cute little asshole, Lou. Sit on my face, Lou. Stick it in my mouth.*

And Lou would read it all out, solemn and scholarly, making his way down the page with his penlight. He read carefully, line by line, his voice even. And the guys would listen and groan deep down inside.

Sometimes Mack would take his knife and stab it into the dirt, flicking up little fountains of grit. "I'm coming. Oh man, I'm coming," he would moan.

Lou would stop reading. "Pay attention now," he would said. "Listen to this."

And on he would go in his steady voice, line by careful line, following them down the page with his penlight.

And then, "That's all for now, folks," and he'd fold it up carefully, looking round at their faces, flashing his penlight onto them one at a time. "That's all for now," he'd say.

After a while the guys began to live for those letters. "Anything from Tammy?" Sal would ask anxiously when the mail was dropped. And they'd all wait while Lou sorted through the sack.

Lou was the honorary mail sorter. He took the place of honor. He'd hand out the letters.

"One for you," he'd say, smiling. "And one for you." Then he'd dig around. "Oh, lucky man," he'd say, "Here's one for you." Passing them out like a ceremony, like he was handing out medals. And they'd all sit down and read.

Letters from home. Letters from girlfriends and mothers. Letters from family. LT always got one from his wife, but he never read it out. No-one read theirs out as a rule, only Lou, and not right then. He'd take his off to the side and read it through slowly. Then he'd turn it over and look at the back of each page. Then he'd read it all through again. He took a long time with his letter, moving his lips over it, looking up now and then and staring off into some image only he could see. When he was done, he'd fold it up and get out the packet and tuck it onto the top under the green rubber band. It didn't get the full red across and green down treatment until it had been read out to everyone. For now he'd snap the green rubber band over it and look around at everyone and smile.

"Later," he'd say.

And everyone would read their own letters

and watch him furtively. Letters from home.

Sal got cover letters from his mother with the sports pages. Dan got letters from his wife, Charlie from Pauline. Mack got them from his kid sister and his mother as well. Once he got a whole packet of letters in a big brown envelope, one from every kid in his kid sister's class at school.

They were strange little letters with pictures of "me and my dog" and "this is my baby brother" on them. Drawings in crayon and pencil and colored in carefully between the lines. One kid sent a drawing of a dinosaur, Tyrannosaurus Rex, with it's mouth open wide and blood dripping off its teeth.

A little boy drew an intricate picture in black pen of tanks and guns and soldiers shooting and bad guys lying dead on the ground. He put an arrow pointing to one of the bodies. "Charlie is dead," it said. But it wasn't right. The bodies were too big and too fat.

There were trenches too, and puffs of artillery smoke and soldiers in metal helmets and up in the sky was the Star Ship Enterprise with long straight lines coming out of its sides zapping at the figures on the ground. There was an arrow pointing to one of the lines. "Death ray," it said.

Mack liked that picture a lot. He showed it around to everyone and then he drew one to send back. Then he turned the kid's picture over and copied the name. Tommy Jergens was the kid's name.

Mack wrote him a letter.

Thanks for the picture, Tommy, he wrote. *Here's one for you. This is what it really looks like here.*

He drew rice paddies and mountains with dotted tunnels all through them and a big helicopter coming in, sweeping the dust up in a cloud, flattening the bushes and making the elephant grass lie down in rows. He drew soldiers on the ground with their backs turned and their shoulders hunched against the stinging dirt and pieces of flying rock sucked up and thrown away by the helicopter. He drew six dead Charlies neatly in a row, one through six, small skinny men with a trail of dotted blood from each one, a leg, a chest, each one dead of a different wound. And standing above them was a single GI with an armored jacket and pieces of bush stuck in his helmet. He held a rifle triumphantly above his head and wore a big grin.

Then Mack drew a bubble coming out of his mouth. "Got the little fuckers!" it said.

There was an argument about that. "You can't send that to a kid," Sal said.

"Hey, what's wrong, man? You don't like my picture?"

"Cain't send it to no eight-year-old kid, man," said Harold T. Booker.

"What's wrong, hey? What's wrong?" Mack turned his picture around and examined it anxiously. "It's a good picture. Dead Charlies. Look at them. A

136

good picture."

"Bad language," said Sal. "Can't send fuckers to an eight-year-old kid. Bad for his moral development. What think, LT?"

LT craned to see. "No," he said. "Can't do it."

"What then? What?"

"Suckers," said LT. "Suckers'll do it."

"Sure. That'll do," said Sal and Harold T. agreed.

So Mack scratched out the fuckers and changed it to suckers and sent it off to Tommy Jergens with the next pick-up.

Charlie lay in his hole in the dark and thought about Tommy Jergens. It took his mind off the itch and the griping of his bowels. He wondered if Tommy had liked Mack's picture. He wondered if he'd shown it around the class to the other kids. He was probably proud of it. A picture from a real soldier. It was enough to make any little kid proud. He wondered if he'd written back or sent another picture.

But he'd never know about Tommy Jergens now, would he? He could make the story up himself. He could make everything up himself lying down here. The truth didn't matter any more. There wasn't any truth or any more reality. Only what he made up in his head and played like a movie in front of his eyes.

He lay still, flat out on the floor, his legs

spread and his arms stretched out, listening to the rhythm of his itching, following the chiggers as they made their paths and tunnels underneath his skin.

When he was a child he once had kept an ant farm. It was the rage. All the children had one. Two pieces of clear glass upright in a green holder and a narrow space with soil between so little boys could see how ants lived. He had watched those creatures hours on end as they made their passages and pathways through the dirt and he had marvelled at their diligence and at the intricacies they built.

He felt he was a man of glass pressed flat against the floor. He watched himself. He watched the chiggers make their intricate paths and tunnels underneath his flesh and listened to his itching. He tracked it, drew the pattern of the pain in the darkness, a yellow graph that surged and peaked and dropped and levelled out. And after a while he could predict the surges, hold his breath until they peaked and faded.

He chewed off all his fingernails, worrying on them until they were down below the quick, to keep himself from scratching in his sleep. He learned to breath in rhythm with the itching and found he could control it. When the surges came he lay there panting like a dog in the dark, watching the graph climb up its mountain, reach the top in triumph and slide down into another trough to climb again. He taught himself to live with it and not go mad.

HOW THEY CUT HIS THROAT

He slept sometimes and he woke sometimes. He itched sometimes and sometimes he was numb, waiting and waiting in the dark, waiting for them to take him west to Hanoi.

But they seemed to have lost interest in him. They didn't come to stare and chatter to each other about him any more and they made no effort to interrogate him. They just kept him alive and left him there.

They still came from time to time, bringing food and water and hauling off his jar once in a while when it threatened to overflow. He always got water but he didn't always get a riceball now. Once it was leaves and sometimes it was nothing. He couldn't eat the leaves. He didn't even try.

"Here, you have them," he said holding them out to Man One. "Is that what you've been living on?"

Man One said nothing but he took the leaves.

"Poor devil," Charlie said. "A sorry way to fight a war."

Charlie didn't care much whether he ate or not because his bowels griped so badly. If he ate they griped. If he didn't eat they griped anyway. They ran constantly and sometimes they exploded in a spray. He worried about where it all came from. He ate almost nothing and he put out more each day than he took in in water. He could feel his body shrivelling up. He must be drying out.

Twice his jar overflowed. Man Two wasn't pleased about it. He muttered angrily and cursed him. It was a Vietnamese curse but a curse is a curse and Charlie recognized it.

After that they took care to haul off his jar more often and replace it with a new one. He knew it was more often but he couldn't tell how often it was because he had long since lost all sense of time. Now everything ran together. It might have been morning or it might have been evening or midday or the dead of night.

It wasn't dead of night, he told himself. They worked at night, out in the haunted jungle; although they hadn't taken him at night, but in the morning, so he really couldn't tell. As far as he could judge, it was twice a day or twice a night. And after a while he couldn't tell at all. They might be coming regularly or they might not.

There was no time down here.

They usually brought a candle with them when they came, sometimes a flashlight, once an oil lantern of some sort. Sometimes they came in the dark.

The flashlight hurt his eyes, and the lantern too, but the candle was very pale and it was all right after he squinted a while, getting used to it. He was becoming a mole, not liking the light, waiting for it to go away again.

He could see with his fingertips better than with his eyes now. His fingertips had told him there was no ventilation shaft, but the pale flicker of the candle on the walls and ceiling of his hole was a will-o'-the-wisp telling him to look, look again, look in this shadow, that one. There were a lot of shadows. Any one of them could have been a ventilation shaft. But his fingertips had been right. There was no ventilation shaft.

He thought about the war stories he had read in his youth, tales of handsome and heroic men who became prisoners of war. The hero would always mark off the days of his captivity on the wall of his prison, six marks upright and one diagonal, with a nail, a spoon, a stone. He should be marking his wall, Charlie told himself. He could do it with his belt buckle. But a mark was no good because he couldn't see and when he tried to make an indentation, the wall crumbled around it.

How long had he been here? A week? A month? A lifetime? Was he old now? Had he become a decrepit old man without realizing how time had passed?

He reached up to feel his head: full of hair still. He felt his neck: no wattle. His chin: he should have been able to tell by his beard but he'd never grown one before and had no idea how fast it would grow. It wasn't long yet but he was not a hairy man and maybe it would never grow long. He felt his cheeks. So bony. His fingers stopped, then felt carefully. His face was coming off.

His stomach heaved. He felt again, touching each part of his face with sensitive fingertips.

It wasn't coming off after all. It was peeling. He took hold of a strand of skin hanging below his cheekbone and pulled at it gingerly. It peeled back to the corner of his eye. He felt the new skin underneath: a little sensitive but it seemed to be whole. He ran the palm of his hand quickly over his cheeks and forehead. The loose skin felt like little flags fluttering all over it.

At least it didn't hurt. He would ignore it, think about something else.

He thought about Man Two, imagined he saw him riding inside the mountain, riding and riding, up and down through the tunnels, a magic cyclist on a magic bicycle. He imagined that he would follow him one day, following, following, until he came to the entrance again and then he would leave and go back to the platoon.

Harold T. Booker would look up and say, "Hey, if it ain't ol' honky Charles. Where you been, white boy? We thought you was dead."

And Dan would smile, "Now," he'd say, "let's see what I've got here in my bag of tricks." And he would open his medic's pouch and take out a shining white tube. "Something for that ugly face of yours," he'd say. "Get it over here and let me fix it for you. And when we've done that we'll get those chiggers out. No call for you to be itching like that."

Charlie wanted to smile to himself but the darkness was heavy on him and his mouth clung heavily to his teeth. An enormous lethargy seemed to have him in its grip. He tried to rouse himself but it swung him down, down inside it, in a heavy, ponderous swirl.

He lay there staring into the blackness. He closed his eyes, opened them again. There was no difference. The blackness sat on his head and stopped him thinking; it sat on his chest and stopped him breathing. It made his body heavy, so heavy the earth could scarcely bear its weight.

And then they cut his throat. They did it while he slept; slid up the entrance to his hole, quiet as death, and slit it ear to ear.

He was not surprised. He wasn't a prisoner of war, after all. He was an interesting creature taken captive by children. They would have tired of him eventually, as children always do, forgotten him most likely, left him to wither and dry out in his cage.

But children are not always forgetful of their captive creatures. Sometimes they are cruel and torture them; sometimes they are brutally dismissive, crushing them with a rock, shaking the cage till they die in a sad spatter against the sides.

So it wasn't surprising that these children had cut his throat.

It was a great pain. His mouth was full of blood. He started to swallow and couldn't. He reached up his hand carefully and felt his throat. It was swollen but he couldn't find the cut. He moved his tongue inside his mouth, reached up a finger and tested the consistency.

It was saliva after all. It was the inside of his throat that hurt so badly. He could feel it, red and raw, swelling up so it blocked his breathing.

He couldn't swallow at all. The spit ran down from one corner of his mouth and onto his chest. He smudged at it with the flat of his hand. It didn't matter. No-one could see him dribbling like a baby in the dark. Soon his throat would be so swollen he couldn't breath. He would die down here in the dark. An American hero. Died of a sore throat. And chiggers.

Man One gave him honey for his throat.

"Very good," he said while Man Two held a rifle at the opening of the tunnel. Charlie could see him crouching there.

Man One held out the honey. "Very good," he said. He was very gentle. He held it out on a stick. "Very good." And Man Two held a rifle on him from the mouth of the tunnel.

The honey was good. It soothed his throat. "Very good," Charlie said.

Man One left him a cut-off can with a little honey in the bottom and a stick to get it out with. It worked. It soothed his throat and the next time he woke he felt better. He put some of the honey on his chigger bites but couldn't tell if it did any good so he used it for his throat and it made it better.

But now his toe was rotting and he wished he hadn't used up all the honey. He asked Man One for more but Man Two made a phlegmy sound of disgust in his throat and Man One turned his hands up empty and left him alone with his toe.

He knew it was rotting. He could smell it in the darkness. The flesh was soft and giving under his toenail. It was long now, the toenail. And the flesh underneath was rotting away.

He stuck it out as far away from him as he could, turning his face away from the smell. But then he got used to it and couldn't smell it any more, just reached out to his long toenail from time to time, pressing it gently into the soft flesh, moving it up and down, softly, painfully, working at it like a loose tooth. If he could get the toenail off, then maybe the infection would dry up.

He wondered if it were gangrene.

He lay there and listened to his toe, one boot

on, one boot within hand's reach, set neatly against the wall of his hole. And when he gave up on his toe, he took off the other boot and set it by the first, neatly, a man arranging a pair of boots against a wall.

It was probably footrot, some sort of tropical mildew growing under his toenail. He could feel it there living off him. He could feel the inflammation underneath it. It itched, a different itch from chigger itch. This wasn't a sharp panicked itch that made you want to tear your flesh off so that it took all your self-control to resist the urge. This was a deep living itch, a backdrop of sensation, like the drip drip of moisture falling down onto the jungle floor. He had a miniature jungle living off him, growing under his toenail there in the dark.

Mack used to call it mung. He suffered from it all the time. "I got mung," he would say. "Dis-gusting." And he would dig at it with his knife.

"You'll do yourself an injury," LT would say, "chopping at your feet like that. You need those things to walk on. Don't chop at them like that."

"I got the mung," Mack would say. "Dis-gusting." And he would hold his knife delicately, just behind the tip of the blade, and slide it up under his toenail. "Dis-gusting."

"Got just the thing for mung," Dan would say, reaching for his medical kit. He would paint Mack's toes red the way he'd painted Harold T.'s balls when he had crotchrot. Crotchrot or footrot, it was all the same. Mung.

Dan never got mung himself. He got dysentery instead. He suffered from it badly. He called it the trots, but it was dysentery. When he got it, Harold T. Booker would start up with his own version of a kid's chant: "Dan, Dan the medical man, all he can do is sit on the can." He used to call him Dysentery Dan and laugh.

Dan didn't think it was very funny when he got it, running sweat and turning inside out at the edge of the trail, hoping the dinks wouldn't get him in the naked ass, and weak as a kitten for days after. But the name was catchy and Harold T. was jovial enough about it and after a while he laughed at it himself in between attacks. He was a good-natured man, a boy really, and he cared for their health like a mother.

"Got just the thing for mung here in my bag of tricks," he would call, opening it up carefully, touching each medical treasure inside with reverent fingers. "Mung medicine. Here you are. Get your ugly feet over here."

Charlie reached down to his toe. The mung was under the right big toenail. He pressed on it carefully in the dark. It was getting more tender to the touch all the time and he could feel the inflammation starting to travel. He twisted up his foot and blew on the toe, to dry it off, dry out the mung. If he could get it good and dry it would go away.

It wasn't dripping wet down here, but it was dank. His own mildew wasn't all there was. The smell of mildew had been rank in the air when he first was down here, but he didn't notice it any more. He didn't smell anything. At first he'd smelled everything: the mildew and the dull thick smell of packed dirt, and his open-necked jar and the feral smell of his own body. But these continuing smells had gone down to the bottom of his senses. He didn't notice them any more, although he noticed new smells.

He smelled the thin musty smell of the riceballs he ate from time to time. And he smelled the water in his canteen because it had a lid and he could hold the smell in there and let it out to please himself.

The water had a strange metallic smell and after it had been down here a while it got warm and smelled sour. He drank it anyway, and sometimes laid it in careful drops on his face and neck, the insides of his wrists and elbows, to cool himself off.

But there was no getting away from the heat. It hung thick and heavy on the air. It had its own smell. The smell of heat.

He smelled the bodies of Man One and Man Two when they came to give him his riceball and renew his water and, from time to time, change the broad squat jar that was his bathroom. That smell had been the last to which he had become accustomed. He had smelled it all the time. The jar had no lid so he had taken off his flak jacket and clamped it down hard on the top to keep the smell in, but nothing kept it in and after a while he grew accustomed to that too and didn't smell it any more. No more sweat, no more stink from his body. No more shit. My shit don't stink.

New smells hit him like a fist though, would wake him out of sleep. Mainly they were Man One and Man Two coming down the tunnel from the outer darkness. He smelled them sometimes before he heard them because they moved like spirits, silent. But he smelled their bodies, a fetid odor like fish out there in the outer darkness.

He could remember smells too, conjure them up. Sometimes he still smelled the honey that Man One had brought for his sore throat. Even though his throat had been raw and swollen so he couldn't swallow, he had smelled the sweet sharp smell of the honey and he could remember it exactly. He would hold it under his nose and inhale the sweetness and smile to himself in the dark.

He could conjure up all sorts of smells: the smell of backyard barbecue, the smell of snow coming, of the air, fresh and crisp after one of the sudden summer storms that used to rush through the Washington evening, making the trees bow down and throw up their hands. He could conjure up the smell of Pauline's hair. And Minh's. Don't think of Minh.

He could conjure up the smell of Oil of Sandlewood, the smell of Tammy's letters.

HOW TAMMY'S LETTERS SMELLED
OF SANDLEWOOD

Dear Lou, Tammy wrote, *Yesterday I went shopping for you. I bought this sexy little outfit that's red with lace around the tops of the legs and peek-a-boo holes in the cups. It's one-piece, like those old-fashioned girdle things women used to wear, the ones with whalebones, but real sexy.*

It's red, like I said, with satin and lace and legs cut so high I had to shave my you-know-what, and cut so low at the top I just about fall out. I put it on just for you, Lou baby...

Mack, who had been jabbing about under his toenails and moaning gently to himself, dropped the knife and fell backwards onto the ground with a smack, panting at the sky.

Lou stopped reading and looked severely at him. "Shut up that noise. You want to hear this or not?"

Mack stopped panting and sat up. "Yessir. Sorry, sir. You go right on, sir. I'm behaving."

Lou looked down and shuffled his letter. Mack looked across at Sal and winked, and Sal made a jerking-off motion.

Lou looked up suddenly but Mack, looking

insouciant, had picked up his knife and was back to picking at his toes with it.

Lou resumed his letter.

And I bought some incense and these fancy oils that you rub all over and they make you smell nice and feel so horny. I wanted to have a picture made but didn't like to ask anyone, because of what they might think, or tell my mom, who would be furious. You know what she's like, Lou, so self-righteous, and you know how people talk too, as if they had nothing better to do than discuss the business of others.

But anyway, you can think of me in it and I'll put it on when you get back and you can rub me all over with this oil. It's called Oil of Sandlewood and the lady in the store said it's the most erotic. And then I'll rub it on you, all over your big hard cock and then we'll get down on the floor and I'll sit on your face and you can...

When Lou read out the last bit, so slow and serious, Mack's knife jerked and he said, "Shit! Look what you've gone and made me do now, Lou."

Harold T. Booker laughed and said, "Look at that. The fool got so hotted up with lust he sliced off his own toe."

Mack examined his toe. "It's not off," he said. "Just cut up a bit."

Dan paid attention to that. "You'd better let me give you something to put on it," he said, reaching for his medical kit. "You'll be getting gangrene if you keep slicing at yourself like that. With this climate, never know what's going to get in there. All sorts of little creatures around in the tropics. You've got to pay more attention."

He fussed around, dabbing Mack's toes, making them dark red. "Anyone'd think I was here to be your mother, messing around all the time with your damn toes. Using up perfectly good stuff intended for when you're lying dying."

Harold T. Booker looked offended. "Now, that ain't a nice thing to say to a man. Say things like that you could put a hex on old Mack. And all he did was get a little overheated. You ought to take them words back afore they do damage."

So Dan took the words back, muttering and bandaging up the damaged toe, and all the while Lou had been going on quietly ploughing his way through the rest of his letter.

"That's all for now, folks," he said, refusing to go back over it. "Hey, you don't pay attention, you don't get the good bits," he said, snapping the rubber bands and looking coy. "You can smell them though."

He passed the packet of letters around. "They smell of sandlewood."

HOW LOU WAS POINT MAN

He still had them, Tammy's letters, in the pocket of his shirt. He wondered why Man One and Man Two hadn't taken them. Perhaps they had looked at them and decided they held no secrets.

But they did hold a secret. They held the secret to why he was down here; and the secret to why Lou was dead, why they were all dead.

They were heavy there in his pocket, pulling his shirt open across his chest. When he took them it had seemed to him there was something he was going to do with them but he couldn't remember what it was now.

He stared into the darkness and looked at Lou, sprawled in front of him with his head ripped off his neck and his arms flung out on the path. He tried to see the others, all dead, but he couldn't. Only Lou, sprawled on the path with the stump of his neck white with the shock of it and his fingers curled upwards like a baby's. And Tammy's letters heavy in his pocket, pulling his shirt open across his chest. A man without a head.

Lou was point man. He was very good at it. He never missed a thing and he never made a mistake. Because of him they didn't see much of Victor Charlie, almost nothing in fact. It wasn't that sort of war for them, wasn't intended to be. But they saw where he had been.

Sometimes they would go for days with nothing but the heat and the leeches and the sudden harsh call of a high bird and the moisture drip, drip, dripping onto the jungle floor, making a noise in the silence like creeping.

Then, out of the blue, Lou would stop, one hand up. "A wire here," he would say, ever so softly, and the men would pass it down the line.

Lou would squat down to examine the wire, tracking it to its deadly source. He never got excited and he never panicked. Just, "A wire here," and the hand held up.

It wasn't always a wire, strictly speaking. Sometimes it was a trip stick or a piece of vine. They were all wires to Lou. Hold up a hand. "A wire here." Then they'd go to work getting rid of the thing.

There were the punji pits too. Sticks, Lou called them. Again the hand held up. "Sticks here," he'd say, coming across a pit. He'd kick some of the leaves and debris off the edge of the cover and then he'd kneel down and examine it carefully.

And the forest would drip, drip all around, soft and deadly.

"They used to use these pits to catch tigers," he told them. "They'd run across the top and fall right through and impale themselves on the sticks. Quite a sight it must have been, don't you think? A full grown tiger snarling and raging down there, his mouth all drawn back and foaming. And those teeth! Can't you just see him? Clawing at the walls of the pit, impaled. Tiger pits they are, fellas. Tiger pits for Yankee imperialists."

There were other sorts of booby traps. Many sorts. Ingenuity went into those traps. Whatever they had they used. Whatever they picked up, things left lying around by the Yankee intruder, they used too.

They were great with bombs. They made bombs from Coke cans and C-ration cans and tobacco cans, any sort of can. Give them a can and they could make a bomb. Have a Coke, lose a head; have a smoke, bang you're dead. The ultimate penalty for littering.

The worst of the small bombs were the ones that jumped straight up out of the ground with no warning to snatch the groin out of a man. Anything that burst and shouted was bad: a man could die as well from his legs ripped off or his head ripped off or his guts ripped out. He could die from any of them. But to have your groin snatched out seemed like an insult too; it made it worse.

They weren't all twentieth century, though, these traps. There were strange, prehistoric cross-bows in the forks of trees and sharpened punji sticks set in the rice paddies below the surface of the water, just the right height for stepping on. They could jam right through a boot and put a man's foot out of action and sometimes they were poisoned, which was worse.

They put punji sticks in streams too, and tripwires that would detonate grenades and jerry-rigged explosives.

Lou avoided streams when he could. "Hard to see a wire in water like that," he would say. He avoided paddies too. "Just don't know what might be under that water," he would say.

Yes, he was good at it. He had a feel for it, a nose for danger. He never missed a one until the flying mudball got him. It only took one slip and it was all over. One slip in concentration.

Tammy did it. What hundreds of Charlies hadn't done, Tammy did. All those miles of jungle, with the trees drip dripping like a soft knocking from hell, all the bad food and the hot sun and the sleepless nights and exhausted days and the dirt and the stink and the chigger bites and the deep mindless fear of death that stalked them through the jungle: none of that did it. Tammy did. She ruined his concentration. Killed him as sure as if she had put a knife in his heart.

And that was what she did. She put a knife in his heart and turned it slowly, slowly. A mad lover who fucked and killed. A preying mantis. She killed him, God curse her soul. She killed them all.

HOW HE WATCHED LOU READ
HIS LAST LETTER

It was the last letter that did it.

Charlie brought his mind carefully to the edge, like a swimmer coming to a winter ocean. He tried the water delicately, stood there watching how it throbbed and heaved beneath its flat grey surface. He broke the flatness in one small spot, a toe in, testing. He backed away from it, kicking at the wet sand at its edge, came back, tried it with his toe again, stepped in gently.

The letter was from Tammy's mother. Lou read it out just the same as he'd read all the rest: in a low level voice with his finger tracking the lines down the page line by line by line. His voice was just the same.

Dear Lou, he read, *I'm sorry to have to be the one to tell you this and I don't rightly know quite how to put it but someone will eventually and it had best be done by someone who cares about you and isn't just some tattle-tale. The truth is, Lou, and I can only tell you straight and blunt, your wife is a whore.*

It's been going on a long time and we all tried to ignore it, hoping it would stop on its own but it hasn't. It's gotten worse in fact and the whole town is talking about it and the preacher gave a sermon on whoring last Sunday at the morning service which is supposed to be reserved for them that are the Lord's and not for them that are wanderers, which is what the evening service is for, so you see he thought it was that important.

I'm so ashamed about this Lou, as it was me and her father that brought her up, but we seem to have failed because it has not just been one man, nor one that she has known a while and fell to temptation unawares, but anyone at all she can get her hands on, strangers.

Her father is in a state and says how will we ever hold up our heads again, with that poor lad off over there fighting for his country and his wife in motels all round town with men she never met before. And there are also rumors that it's not just been in motel rooms but in public places as well, like down by the river and in the river too. Once I even heard of it in the city park, in the bushes. Another time it was on that ledge that runs around the top of the old quarry and can be looked down on from the back road should anyone passing happen to turn their eyes that way.

I just don't know what could have come over her, Lou, and now the worst part is she finally got herself in the family way and told no-one, not a soul, just took herself off to some evil man, not a real doctor of any sort, and between them they did away with the child.

That's when it all boiled up to a head and came out into the open, you see, Lou. She got real sick and bled like a stuck pig and we thought she would surely die for her *sins.*

She's all right now though and begs us not to tell you because if no-one tells you then there's no reason for you to ever know. But her father and me, we agreed, Lou, that it's only right and proper you should know about something like this. A woman that will kill her own child!

We would have raised it for her, Lou. It was our grandchild no matter who the father. We would have loved it. How could she kill her child? It isn't natural that a woman should hate her child like that, enough to kill it. I cannot understand it. I asked her about it. Didn't you love the little thing at all? I asked her. Not at all, she said. She has no remorse. I cannot understand it.

She hasn't left you, Lou, but she's soiled goods and it's up to you whether you want to have anything more to do with a woman who would treat you in such a way and not love her own child.

I have cried myself dry over this and her father has become an old man. He has taken it real hard, him being a god-fearing man and a deacon in the church a full twenty-five years, and now his only daughter that he set such store in has shamed him in front of all the congregation. He blames himself and wakes up in the night crying out, God forgive me! God forgive me! And his eyes are awful to see.

It is a hard time for us all, Lou, and as I said, we thought it right to tell you before someone else told you in spite. I'm sorry, Lou.

When he was done there was silence; none of

the usual groans, no requests for rereads, no remarks about jism. Silence.

Everyone had found something to stare at. Sal was staring at the end of his rifle, scrunching it about in the dirt. Mack stared intently at the radio as though he expected some word of advice to come rattling out of it. Harold T. Booker stared at Mack's boot with engrossed interest. Dan closed his eyes and stared at the inside of his head, and LT stared at a spot in the air an inch or so in front of his face. Charlie stared at Lou.

"So she's slept around a bit," said Mack suddenly, still staring into the radio. "It's not so bad."

"Yeah," said Harold T. Booker to Mack's boot. "It ain't so bad. Ain't one of you haven't done the same some time or other."

There was silence again. Even the jungle seemed to hold back on its steady weeping.

"But she's a woman," said Sal. "There's a difference."

Harold T. Booker lost interest in Mack's boot and looked at Sal. "Hey! Man, woman. So you sleep around a bit. What's the difference?"

"Big difference, man."

"What is it, then?"

Sal laid his rifle flat on the ground and met his gaze directly. "Women get pregnant, man. Men don't."

"He's right on that," said LT to the air in front

of his face. "The difference." He looked sad.

There was silence again and one by one their eyes turned to Lou.

Lou ignored them all. He brushed away a fly from near his eye and folded his last letter carefully, the way he had folded all the others. He reached inside his shirt and took out the bundle with its red across and green down, snapped off the rubber bands and laid them carefully side by side on a leaf. It was a palm leaf and the red and green circles made a pattern on its vertical slashes. He set the letter on top of the pile, tapped them smartly on his knee to get them straight, as he always did, and picked up the red rubber band.

They all watched him going through the familiar pattern of movements they had watched so often with interest, amusement, fascination, boredom hot with sexual desire. They watched now the pattern of his pain. Snap. Snap. Red across, green down.

"That's all for now, folks," said Lou, not looking at them. "Time to move." And then he said an odd thing: "Kill or be killed," he said. He reached for his rifle, point man again.

He should have known right then, Charlie told himself. He should have seen it. He had sat there with his hands dangling between his knees, watching the pattern of Lou's pain. Snap. Snap. Red across, green down. But he'd missed the import of it.

He should have noticed something like that. He could have had a word with LT. They could have moved Lou off point that morning. They could have moved him to the middle of the column where he would have been protected, where he could have nursed his hurt. If he'd just said something, LT would have moved someone else up front to point. He could have done it himself.

But he'd missed it. They all had. They'd gone off through the jungle with a deadly wound at point. A wound that killed them all.

Charlie stepped back suddenly from thinking of it. The water there was cold and very deep. Too cold and deep. He turned his back on it.

He tried to keep his mind on other things but the rip was pulling hard now. He mustn't sleep or it would take him.

To keep himself awake, he crawled down the access tunnel to the bars and back. He did that a dozen times or more and then he crawled around his hole, around and around, and then around the other way. He talked to himself and sang to himself and drank from his canteen and thought about Pauline. He stayed awake a long time.

Then black sleep took him unawares and the water rose around him in the dark. It surged up swift and sudden and pulled him down into a freezing embrace.

He dreamed that he was on the path again, flat on his belly, one hand raised up towards the basket with its grisly load. It was big, the basket so packed with mud that a man's arms could not have encircled it, and shot through with stakes so honed and sharpened it could take a man's head right off his body.

And it had: a gigantic mace with razor edges swinging down with all the force of gravity. It ripped Lou's head right off his neck, impaled it on its downward plunge and bore it off to ride amongst its daggers while it ripped on through the line of fragile men.

Charlie forced himself to look.

Lou's head was turned to one side as though he had seen it coming and turned his head away. His ear nestled against the great ball, his eyes were vacant and his mouth ajar, as though listening to a great truth that spoke its name inside.

Charlie reached his hand up toward the spikes and looked into Lou's face.

"What is it, Lou old buddy? What do you hear in there?"

And Lou opened his eyes and looked at him.

"Tammy," he said.

"It's me, Lou. Charlie."

"It's all one," Lou said very softly. "All one." And the words went into Charlie's heart with such force that he jerked as though he had been shot; but he didn't understand their meaning. He looked long and hard into Lou's face and then turned suddenly away; and the water swept up around him, cold as death.

He woke with his heart racing in his chest and very cold. The dream hung before his eyes like a picture hung on a wall and Lou's words came out of it and echoed in his head.

"All one," he said. "All one."

Charlie shivered so he couldn't stop. He huddled down inside his shirt, chilled in his oven hole. It had got him then, the mosquito. He hadn't killed it. He told himself that if he could just remember the incubation period for malaria he would have some idea how long he'd been down here. He racked his brains but he couldn't remember anything but Lou's ghastly head telling him, "All one. All one."

He didn't understand it. There was a meaning that he couldn't find. The picture hung before his face, insisting. "All one," it said. "All one." What was the meaning? It was very important that he know. If he could find the meaning, he told himself, he would be free. He looked inside himself but he found nothing there but cold confusion.

He felt ill. The muscles of his neck and shoulders twisted into spiked balls of pain and the top of his head clanged open and shut. The chills made his teeth rattle and he clenched his jaw, trying to hold them still, afraid they would fly out of his head when the top came off.

There were lights in the blackness, red flashing lights and quick sharp streaks of white, tiny multicolored dancing spots. He shook his head to dislodge them but his teeth flew around like a hailstorm and pinged off the inside of his skull and the colors flashed behind them, blending with each other like a night scene on a slow film. He curled in on himself and clung hard, staying very still, feeling the blood freeze in his veins, becoming rigid, carved in ice.

Then his head clanged open again and a hot wind surged down through his skull. His body opened up in relief but the wind had lit a furnace in his skull and his teeth were melting, running down through his veins, boiling the frozen blood, running down through the burrows and passageways dug by the chiggers, driving them into a frenzy. He dug his fingernails into his chest and ripped at the flesh, making a place for the flaming chiggers to escape; but they wouldn't come out. They ran furiously around, digging deeper, burning their way into his liver, his kidneys, all his vital organs. He was on fire. He thrashed on the ground, beating at the flames, rolling into the walls of his hole, burning his hands putting out the fire.

Again his head clanged open and a great torrent of water rushed through it, flashing to steam, making his tongue swell and heave in his throat. The water kept coming, boiling off in great hissing clouds, filling his hole with such a dense hot vapor he couldn't breathe, rushing down his body like monsoon rains down a mountain, putting out the fire, welling up around him, rocking him.

Man One and Man Two were talking to each other. They were discussing him. They went on a long time, sharp metallic words going back and forth. Then they went away.

He was glad they had gone. It was peaceful, tucked away here in his hole, away from the noise and suddenness of war. He was protected by the earth, like a mother's womb, warm and safe and dark. He pulled the darkness around him like a blanket and let the water hold him, float him gently away through the trapdoor in his head.

HOW THERE WAS NO FORGIVENESS

When he woke, he was sprawled in the sun at the water's edge. He could see the glow on his closed eyes and the light fed energy into his tired body. For a moment he thought he was back on the beach at Danang but when he listened for the rush and ripple of waves the water was still and silent and he knew that he was somewhere else that wasn't in Danang or Vietnam or even in the world.

It was pleasant here and warm and very light. If he could just open his eyes he could stay here forever and there would be no more darkness. He struggled with his eyelids but they stayed tightly closed.

At last he gave up the effort. He turned his face up to the healing light, lay spreadeagled underneath the sun. And as he lay there he heard a wind come out of the sun, high up and far away. It swept across the golden sky, coming closer and closer, and Charlie knew that this was death. When it was very close he heard horses galloping in the wind.

The sky darkened and his eyelids were released. He saw that he was at the mouth of a trail that led off into the jungle. A cold hand touched his heart; this was the trail where Lou had died and all the others with him. There was death down there and the horses of death were in the sky and coming through the jungle. They rushed towards him, trampling the ferns and grass and mosses with their thundering hooves, laying flat the great trees and trailing the vines behind them, pounding across him as he lay there. If he could just seize one by the mane he could ride with them in the wind to the ends of the universe.

He reached up his hand as they passed above him and they surged around him with their eyes rolling and the muscles of their flanks pumping and pumping; and then they were gone in the distance and all that was left was the sigh of a fading wind.

Charlie lay there a long time, stunned, and then he stood up and made his way along the trail. Lou was down there, just around the bend, with his head impaled on the spikes. He would find him and ease his head away from the great ball and put it back on his body. He would whisper to him, "It's okay, buddy. Okay now. Tammy can't hurt you any more." And then he would ask him the meaning of his dream.

He listened fearfully as he made his way through the undergrowth but all he heard around him was the soft silence of an empty jungle.

Lou wasn't there at the bend in the trail and the giant spiked ball was not there either. He looked at the ground where Lou's body had lain with its pale neck and his fingers curled, and there on the ground was a single flower. It gleamed and shimmered like glass in the dimness. Its colors were more than the colors of the rainbow and so bright that the sight of it was an unbearable ecstacy.

Charlie felt his mind grow large, as though it could encompass all things, and a great truth hovered just above his head. If he could hold the flower in his hand he would know it. But as he reached for it the flower exploded into a thousand tiny spots of brilliance and was gone; and he was overwhelmed with the knowledge that he had sinned a great sin.

"It's all one," Lou had said so sadly with his ear pressed up against the mudball. "All one." And now, kneeling here on this deserted jungle trail, Charlie understood his meaning.

He had been a god, having the power to take life, which is a great power, and to give it, which is greater. And the greater of these powers he had abused, loving falsely and in deceit creating for himself a son to be abandoned. And he knew that his sin and Tammy's were the same.

He flung himself down on the trail and wept. "I'm sorry, Lou," he said. "Sorry I hurt you so."

But there was only silence in the jungle and no forgiveness; and Charlie knew he must go back to his hole, back to the darkness, until he had atoned for his sin. He lay there on the path and wept for Lou and for

Tammy and for the son he did not love; and his tears became a torrent, flooding the jungle.

He came up slowly from a deep dark place, not of his own volition but as though some great pressure forced him upwards.

It was a difficult journey and very long. He felt that he was coming through a pipe or a tube. Its sides were neither hard nor soft but viscous and pulsating as though his passage were through some living thing that, rebelling at this foreign traveller in its gut, clamped its muscles tightly down on him to stop him moving.

The pressure from behind was from the same creature. It fought against itself, straining to expel him while at the same time straining to hold him in. It was as though life and death struggled together in its gut. Life strained to give him birth, while death resisted.

His consciousness was black and senseless at the beginning of the journey and he was pushed and pressured, unresisting.

As the pressure grew, his consciousness grew with it and he turned his awareness upwards as a man coming up from deep water will look upwards to the white sheet of the surface. His ears roared and whirred with a gigantic machine-like sound and he fancied he heard voices calling out of it.

His body hurt. He feared that he would burst

apart from the pressure or else be compacted down into a tiny thing. He felt he was a turd in a blocked bowel, a child crushed in a woman who could not give birth.

The pressure on his head grew like the tightening of a vice until he heard the bones move and overlap each other with a peculiar snapping sound. The pressure from below pushed him up inside himself and pushed and pushed until his body was all forced up inside his head, and pushed and pushed. His head exploded. He cried out with the pain.

Then it was done and he was back. He lay there gasping, his heart heaving in his chest and his wits all askew inside his head. He felt himself all over in a panic to see if he was shaped the same as he had been or if he was now a distorted monster. His head he felt first because it still hurt a great deal and he was sure it was shattered. But no, it was a solid head as always. He felt his neck and shoulders and down across his ribcage, his pelvis and his thighs and legs and feet and then his toes. His toe was rotten still and there was nothing new about the rest except that he felt very thin and bony, more so, it seemed, than before the fever.

He wondered how long it had lasted. He had died, he told himself, not believing it. He had died, he told himself again. He argued with himself about it and then he gave it up because the other matter was beating on his brain, the matter of his son. He understood the meaning of his dream now.

Every sort of guilt leaped out at him, pointing angry accusing fingers at him in the darkness. He submitted to them all. He gave himself to anguish, berating himself for his selfishness and his thoughtlessness and his unkindness and his hardness of heart and the way he had used others and the way he had so easily blamed them for his own misconduct and condemned them when he was no better—worse—himself. He told himself he had cheated Pauline and blamed her for it. He had cheated Minh and blamed her too. And he had cheated his son and blamed him worst of all. He was a worthless, wicked man.

He went on in this fashion for a long time. He suffered like Prometheus, clawing out his own heart and eating it over and over again. He wallowed in his guilt and there was no end to his remorse. He loved his pain.

At last he fell into a deep blank depression and after that self-pity took him over. He cried and grizzled to himself and said, Why me? I don't deserve this, it's just not fair, I didn't realize, I didn't mean...and other things of a similar nature. Then he slept and when he woke he had recovered something of his senses. He began to turn the situation over in his mind.

He was convinced he must atone. But how? Down here, what was to be done? He could pray for forgiveness and if he did then maybe he would be forgiven and maybe not, but there would still be the matter of atonement. He turned it over and over in his mind and puzzled greatly. He slept again and woke and slept and woke and puzzled on.

HOW HE COULDN'T FIND THE ANSWER
TO A RIDDLE

He could smell chicken. Forget it, he told himself. It's nothing but imagination. But no, he really could smell chicken. Well then, his nervous system had started to malfunction. It was only to be expected. This must be the beginning of the end. Not so bad, he told himself, for a man to die with the smell of chicken in his nostrils.

And then he heard them coming and it was chicken after all.

It turned out not to be much, a skinny leg, boiled and limp. But Man One carried it like a prize.

"Eat," he said, the candlelight flickering on his face. "You eat. Be strong. Soon you go west."

Charlie rubbed at his eyes, blinded by the pale limp flame, and ate obediently, surprised that he was hungry at all. But then it was only a few bites and no more hunger.

It had been like this since the fever: his hunger had gone away. Even the thought of eating now made him feel heavy and when he felt heavy the pain returned, the unbearable itching and the throbbing of his rotten toe. His head would hurt then too, making him afraid that it would split open and spill him out again.

He had a new pain as well now, in his chest where he had torn it to let the chiggers out. It hadn't healed. He pulled open his shirt and showed it to Man One.

Man One flared his nostrils and then pressed them together, and Charlie realized that the wound in his chest had begun to stink. He peered down at it curiously but it was just a dark lumpy mass in the dim light.

"It's infected," he said calmly, as though it belonged to someone else.

Man One grunted. "Eat," he insisted. "Soon you go west."

Charlie ate some more. He stuffed it in, his stomach revolting at the richness of the bland meat. "When am I going?" Perhaps he must atone by undergoing torture.

Man One didn't answer him and they didn't take him west and he didn't mind any more.

He lay quietly, listening to his body. It had changed since the fever but he wasn't sure how. He told himself again that he had died and come back to life and then he told himself again that it had all been a delusion. But delusion or reality, the notion of atonement possessed him. He had abandoned his son and there was something he must do about it. He had a growing feeling that his son was facing trouble and needed his father's help. But what to do? He had to think it out. He had to help his son.

A thousand times he asked himself the same questions and a thousand times he found no answers to them: How could he do anything for his son while he was down here? How could he help him? What could he do? What if he died, what then?

He dreamed constantly that he went looking for him at the house in Danang. Sometimes the house was empty and the door fallen off its hinges, or else he knocked and strangers came to the door with fearful eyes. There was some commotion in the air that had no definition. He panicked and turned to run but the little urchin in the baggy pants stood in his way, mocking him.

His head became confused and bewildered, churning questions over and over.

In all this he felt no love for his son and this bothered him too. He told himself that it had been a sin to abandon him but his first sin had been not to love him. He looked inside himself for love but found none. He looked for the image of his son and could not find that either. He was gone and lost, hidden somewhere in the tunnels of his mind.

He told himself that if he could teach himself to love his son then he would be able to find him, and after that he told himself that if he could find him he could teach himself to love him.

And then he came full circle, asking himself, How can I find him when I am down here?

The only way to find him, he told himself, was to get out of here. But he was here because he had sinned. It was his punishment. He must be here and he must go and help his son. He must be in his hole and out of it at the same time. It was a riddle; he had to solve a riddle.

Charlie puzzled mightily over it. He followed each side carefully, looking at it like two sides of a coin, and the more he looked the more he became convinced that it could be done. After all, he told himself, a riddle always has an easy answer once the secret of it is known. He must look for the secret.

He stared into the dark, looking for a place to start but the only thing he was sure of was that his body had changed since the fever and he didn't know how. It was a place to start though. He would start there. If he concentrated very hard he would know what had changed. He turned his mind entirely inward and watched himself.

He lay flat on his back, watching, watching. He tracked the pattern of the tunnels under his skin, tacking the image up in front of his eyes, examining it, looking for a way out. But there was none. He tossed the image away, looked inward again, looking at the itch.

And then he found a peculiar thing. There was no longer him lying there itching; there was only itch. It seemed to Charlie that there was something very significant about this discovery so he turned his attention to his toe and then his chest and found the same thing. There was not him with a throbbing toe; there was only throbbing. There was not him with a burning chest; there was only burning. And when the itching and the burning and the throbbing all came together, there was nothing but a burning, itching, throb.

He was nothing but a bundle of sensations. There was no distinction between him and the world around him. They were one. He was merged with the world and mingled in its particles.

He began to explore this new world of his and found he had made a mistake. He was not trapped down here at all; that was a tale he had told himself, putting words together to imprison himself inside the earth.

"Here I am," he had said, "inside the earth."

But that was wrong. There was no inside the earth or outside. He had taken the words and made himself a prison out of them. He wasn't trapped by the earth; he was trapped by his words. Freedom would come from letting go of the words. He would let them go and then he would be free. He would travel out into the world.

"But there is solid earth around you," said his words.

He must cast them aside, no longer believe in them, release himself from the thrall of language, and go out of here.

Charlie felt all this intensely, like a great revelation, and he began to work at it. But letting go of words was not easy. He found himself seizing at them, clinging to them, not knowing how to relax his grip. Still, he worked diligently at his task.

And then one time Man One came alone. He crouched in the darkness outside the bars and said nothing, waiting.

Charlie felt him there rather than heard him. He smelled him too, a sharp pointed smell that caught in his throat for a moment and then vanished, suffocated by the heavy air inside his hole.

He had been lying flat on his back, not moving, taking each image as it strode into his mind, and peeling off its label. He tossed away the names of things, threw them in a pile, and watched as the image lost its form and wandered for a while before it slowly rose and drifted off and vanished. And he felt that with each one a little part of him went too. He worked at it steadily, one word after another, making his way out.

He came alert as though from a deep sleep, with the kind of feeling that comes from a sound heard and lost with wakefulness. For a full minute he lay there running his senses over this new presence.

"Hi," he said at last.

"Hi," from a hole in the darkness.

There was silence again.

Perhaps it was time to go west. The thought filled Charlie with sudden energy. He twisted himself into a crouch and shuffled his way into the low access tunnel, made his way down it on his elbows and belly. It took a long time because he went carefully, keeping his chest off the ground and pushing with one foot only, to protect his rotten toe. He stopped at the bamboo grid, propping his torso on his elbows, putting up his antennae.

"What's happening?"

"Nothing happen," from the darkness.

Charlie sensed a sudden shyness come over Man One. It confused him for a moment.

Then, "What's the weather like outside?"

There was a small, indeterminate noise from the darkness.

"Much rain," said Man One. "Is the monsoon."

"Ah, yes. The monsoon."

Silence again.

"Pretty damp country, Vietnam."

There was a stirring of interest.

"Dump?"

"Damp. Wet. Raining."

"Ah, damp."

Man One wanted to practice his English. It dawned on Charlie like a light on the horizon. He was about to become a captive teacher, a language instructor in a cage. So much for letting go of words.

Confronted with the notion of a real conversation, the idea seemed suddenly ridiculous. He leaped after language like a drowning man after a life preserver.

"English has many words that mean the same," he said. "They're called synonyms."

Synonyms. The word sang inside his head.

"Syn-o-nyms."

"Yes. Like big and large and enormous, gigantic. They all mean big."

He could feel Man One's mouth closing around the words in the dark. "Enorms. Gi—"

"E-nor-mous. Gi-gan-tic."

Charlie was gigantically, enormously happy. He had thought that by getting rid of words he was making his way to freedom. But he had been wrong. He had been making his way to oblivion. Man One had saved him.

HOW HE TAUGHT MAN ONE ENGLISH

And so began the English lessons.

Like a toy rearranged on a shelf, Charlie seemed to hold a new fascination for Man One. And he found the words coming in a flood. He savored each one as it came out of his mouth. He built them, one after the other, into little piles, like a child playing with blocks, making ideas with them, making worlds, thrilled by their creative power.

He was astonished at himself. He was a new man. He had never talked so much in his life, had never been a talker. But here in the dark with this enemy child he told his whole life. And Man One dutifully repeated it all after him in a strange echoing conversation.

Charlie told him of his youth and how he had been the star catcher of the baseball team, once leaping nearly three feet into the air to make the catch that won the game and took the team to the championships. He told about the first time he fell in love and how he had been teased by his friends all through his three week passion for a skinny girl who ignored him. He told about his grandfather and how he used to take him coyote hunting in the caliche rock-strewn hills of Texas and camp out with him at night and tell him stories of American heroes. He told about his father, who said nothing and wore a big silver belt buckle with a lump of turquoise the size of a hen's egg.

"Turquoise?" said Man One.

"Yes. It's a semi-precious stone. Like gold only not so valuable. It's blue. Bright blue. Like the sky."

"Sky," said Man One.

So Charlie told him about the Indians and how they made jewelry and what had happened to them when the white man came to America and he told about Christopher Columbus and the revolution against the British and George Washington's wooden teeth. He told about the history of the world, about cave men and ancient Egypt and Alexander the Great and Julius Caesar and Adolph Hitler and how the Japanese had bombed Pearl Harbor and the great depression and how President Kennedy had been shot in Dallas. He told about movies too, and television. He told him how John Wayne was a cowboy and Elizabeth Taylor the most beautiful woman in the world. He told him about music and how it could be scratched into a circular piece of plastic.

"It's called a record. Re-cord."

"Le-cord."

"No. Re-cord."

"Le-cord."

"Very good."

Then he told him about Bob Dylan and about the Beatles. "The Beatles are my favorite," he said, and sang him one of their songs. "She was just seventeen," he sang, "If you know what I mean . . ."

"She was just seventeen," Man One sang after him, his voice puzzled.

Charlie told him about science and technology. He told about how men had walked on the moon and about flush toilets and televisions and electric razors and refrigerators.

Man One ignored the moon completely and he didn't understand about refrigerators. Charlie could feel his incomprehension reach out of the darkness like a reproving finger. So he told him about snow and how it fell down out of the sky, and Man One was astonished.

Then he told him about hamburgers and McDonald's french fries and backyard barbecues. He gave Man One the recipe for his special barbecue sauce.

"Put in lots of hot peppers," he said. "And two spoons of honey."

"Two spoons of honey," said Man One obediently.

"I'll teach you to talk like an American now," said Charlie. "Say, uh-huh. That's an all-American word."

"Uh-huh."

"That's yes. Now let's try no. Say, nope."

"Say nope."
"No. Nope."
"Nope."
"That's good. Try Charlie with an ell. Charlie."
"Chah-ree."
"No. Lee. Say lllll."
But Man One couldn't do it. Charlie laughed.
"Okay, we'll work on that."

Man One came back time after time and Charlie talked and talked. He told him about America. He told him about freedom and individual liberty and the rights of man, about the Constitution and the Bill of Rights, leading him step by step through each one. And he told him about the American political system, reaching for a simple way to say it all. He taught him as he would teach a son. And he told him how he loved his country.

"Do you love Vietnam?" he asked. "What is it you fight for? Is it freedom?"

"Freedom," said Man One, but it was an echo, not an answer to his question.

Charlie had two things he puzzled over now. He puzzled about his son and how to help him and he puzzled about Man One too. He wondered where he could have picked up English. He must have done something in his life other than haunt the jungle by night and hide in tunnels in the day. He must have known someone who taught him or at least he must have been around someone who spoke English a lot and picked it up by chance. But how could he have picked up the English he had and yet know so little? He was like a tiny child, having words without comprehension.

Sometimes Charlie was not sure that Man One understood anything of what he said to him in lessons. Indeed, if these were lessons he was giving, they were very odd lessons. The teacher talked; the student listened.

Other times Charlie was sure he understood. There wasn't the give and take of conversation that might be expected in a language lesson, but Man One listened with such intensity of concentration that it seemed impossible he didn't understand. Yes, there was communication between them, he was sure of it, although it wasn't words. It was more a sensitivity in the air, like the wordless playing of a musical instrument. Charlie found a comfort in it.

"What is your name?" he asked Man One softly.

There was no answer. He had asked the question many times before and it was always silence. Man One wouldn't say.

"Tell me your name," Charlie whispered again and this time he felt a stirring in Man One that seemed to be fear, as though giving Charlie his name might give him some strange power over him, some knowledge that could be deadly.

Charlie didn't ask again. One day he would know, but for now Man One would have to do.

Still Man One came back and back, as though drawn to Charlie by a powerful magnet and Charlie looked forward to his coming and planned lessons and stories to tell to this strange student who listened so hard, sucking in the words like a starving man sucking in a bowl of noodles. His concentration was immense. Charlie could feel it out there in the dark, bearing down on every tidbit offered, snatching it out of the air and swallowing it whole.

But nothing came back during these lessons that was made from the words Man One swallowed. He repeated diligently, laboriously. What Charlie said, he said, in bits and pieces, words, sentences, sometimes several sentences strung together, songs. But they were all echoes. There was nothing new created out of all those words. If Charlie asked a question, Man One would repeat it.

The only questions Man One asked were repetitions.

"Touchdown?" he would say, or, "Chevy?"

Charlie had no way to know from his words if he understood but there was no doubt that they communicated.

Indeed, there was a sense in which Charlie grew to know Man One more intimately than he had ever known another person, better than he knew himself. He knew the drumming of his pulse and the flicker of his eyelids in the dark. He knew the way he sucked his front lips through the gap in his teeth when he was excited; the way he tucked his chin back into his neck with a tiny popping sound of disbelief; the way his brain churned and churned inside his head, grinding away at the strange new words funnelling into it. He knew the way his gut churned too, rumbling with a painful hollow sound; he knew his breathing and the faint deep rasping of his lungs; he knew the mucous in his nasal cavities, the saliva in his mouth.

He didn't know his heart though. He knew his heartbeat but he didn't know his heart. Sometimes he thought he did. Sometimes he thought he felt a softness reach out from him. Affection? Love, maybe? Or merely kindness? Sometimes it was a hard pointed stick of some dark black emotion. Hatred? Scorn? He couldn't tell. He told himself that if he could know his name then he would know his heart.

But Man One wouldn't tell.

HOW HE TOLD MAN ONE HIS HEART

Charlie's bones grew so heavy that the earth groaned under their weight. Soon they would sink down beneath its surface and be consumed in its fiery heart. He watched as they grew denser and denser, dragging his fragile body down with them.

Sometimes he didn't itch any more and there were times when he couldn't feel his burning chest either, or his rotten toe.

Once he felt for his toe in the dark and found that the toenail had dropped off. For a while he felt around on the floor of his hole, trying to find it. He would put it back on his toe, where it belonged.

But he couldn't find it. He crawled around the floor, running his hands here and there, but it had vanished, just like the ventilation shaft and Man Two's bicycle. It was magic. The earth had opened up and swallowed them all.

He taught English and American culture to Man One and he lay on the ground and planned what he would teach him next, looking forward to the next time he would materialize silently outside his hole. Those were his happy times.

In his sad times he thought about his son and

tried to figure out the riddle of how to be in his hole and out of it at the same time. He had thought he had the answer and he had been wrong; but still he felt that if he could discover what it was about his body that had changed since the fever, he would solve the puzzle.

His food was the same riceball as before, when he got food. But he didn't eat, couldn't. He tried but the food seemed to fall right though his body and sit heavily on his bones, weighing him down, so he gave up. He drank though with an unquenchable thirst, draining the canteen every time Man One and Man Two filled it up.

The riceballs collected in a sad little pile on the floor of his hole and Man One began to reprimand him about it.

"Eat," he would say, his voice urgent.

Man Two would flick the end of his rifle and speak angrily to Man One, the words rattling out of his mouth like a hail of bullets.

But Charlie didn't eat and he wondered why Man Two was so angry these days. Was it because Man One came alone to visit him? Did he feel left out? Or was it because the war was going badly?

He pulled himself onto his haunches and pressed his ear against the roof of his hole, crouched there listening for the war. Sometimes he thought he could hear a rumbling overhead, fancied that the earth shook; but then it was nothing after all and there was only the imponderable silence.

Sometimes Man One came for his English lesson now and Charlie would lie on the floor of the hole and feel him out there and his bones would be so heavy he could not move at all. He would struggle and heave at them but no, there would be no English lesson that day.

If Charlie came to the bars, Man One stayed and had his lesson; and if he didn't come, he simply went away. More and more he went away.

On these times, Charlie sensed within himself a growing desperation, as though he were losing something gradually. He feared that he was dying and that he would be dead again before he found his son. He feared, too, that he would die and never know Man One's real name. It seemed important.

He tried his best to stir himself to move when Man One came but managed it less and less often. When he did, he talked and talked, hardly knowing what he said, as though he must say everything he knew and felt before it was too late. He lay on his belly and held onto the bars and confessed to everything he had ever done, all he had ever thought, good and bad.

He told everything from the time he cheated in grade school and how he had been found out to the time he shot an old man hidden in a basket of rice and how he had thrown up, giving no weight to one or another but telling them all as one, urgently, re-morsefully. He told about how he shot the sniper in the tree and how the sniper's hands had hung down off his arms like a child's and how he had cried to see them hanging and had clung to the sniper's tree and cried and cried with self-pity and not like a soldier, making a spectacle of himself and taking other soldier's minds off what they should have had them on, the enemy, and although they were not surprised by the enemy while they stood around with their mouths open and watched him in the tree, they could have been, which is just as bad an offence for a soldier, taking his fellows' minds off the enemy. Because that is what gets a soldier killed, not being alert for the enemy. Then he told about Lou and how his head had been ripped off his shoulders and how he could have saved Lou from it if he had thought. And he wept there in the darkness for Lou, and for the others who had died, and for all those he had killed.

One time, night or day he did not know, Charlie spoke into the darkness of Pauline, who was his wife, and his love for her, and he told about his infidelity to her; and he told, too, about Minh and how she had thought she was his wife and how he had deceived her.

And at last he got to the bottom of his heart and told about his son, his Vietnamese son. He told of the pain he had brought on himself because he did not love him and now he could not find him. He tried to work out a way to go and find him and to be in his hole at the same time, taking first this side and then the other, turning it over and over, hopelessly, uselessly; and no matter how he twisted and turned, he always came back to the same question: how can I be here and yet not here?

He told Man One that he was a kind person, a good person, and he had hurt his own child. And yet, if he could discover how to help him, then he would hurt his wife Pauline. How could he choose between them?

"Which one should it be?" he asked the presence outside his cage.

"Which one?" came the echo out of the dark.

HOW HE BECAME LIGHTLY ATTACHED
TO HIS BONES

He didn't sleep any more, he thought; or, if he did, he could no longer tell the difference between sleeping and waking.

Once he thought he dreamed of Pauline.

He stood in her room off the veranda at the back of the house and watched her. She was sitting on the edge of her bed. She sat very still and looked sad. Her hands were in her lap and she stared out the window with an unseeing gaze.

Charlie could see her thoughts swirling around her head, all confused and mixed up together. He saw himself in them, and her, and snatches of things they had done together. And he saw her reading a letter. She held it in her hand and, in the phantasm, tears rolled down her cheeks. He looked at her real self and saw that she was crying too.

She seemed to sense him there and turned towards him.

"Oh, there you are, Charlie," she said, in her practical, unastonished way. "Are you dead?"

She stood up and came across the room to him and made as if to lay her hand on his arm. He felt it move through him like a cool wind.

"Yes, I see you are." She turned away.

Charlie reached towards her, not knowing how to comfort her.

Then he saw the familiar setting of the shoulders, the straightening of the spine. She turned back to him and reached for his hand. He watched it move down through his.

"This won't do at all, Charlie," she said firmly. "You have to come back. No two ways about it. You have to find a way to come back. It is your duty to me."

She smiled at him, her old familiar smile, and he remembered how he had loved her for so long and then had let her down.

"Pauline, forgive me," he whispered.

She looked closely at him, watching his lips as though she were lip-reading.

"I have a son. A Vietnamese son."

He watched her face but she didn't flinch at all.

"Then you have a double duty," she said.

"He is lost."

"Ah." She looked down sadly. "Poor little boy."

"What shall I do, Pauline?"

She turned her face to his, a practical woman. "Why, Charlie, you must find him, of course. What else?"

"How can I do it?"

"I cannot tell you how, Charlie. You are different now—you have a different body—and must discover that for yourself. But you will do it, Charlie. I know you will." She smiled a gentle, reassuring smile and then he couldn't see her any more.

He blinked his eyes and found that they were staring open. He hadn't been asleep, he told himself. It hadn't been a dream. It was too real for dreaming. It was as though the darkness of his hole had become alive and turned into another place. He shivered, feeling that it was a very odd thing to dream like that, so real and present. And what did Pauline mean? "You have a different body," she had said.

He did know that his body was different somehow, but she had said he had a different body. How could this be? Was he dead?

He thought about the time he died—he was convinced now that he had—and asked himself if he were dead again. But no, it was different. He could feel his body and the walls of his hole, and if he pressed down on his chest, the wound was very painful.

He wasn't dead, he told himself, and wondered if he were mistaken. He waited for Man One to come again. If he came again, then he would know for sure.

He came.

"Am I alive?" Charlie asked him.

Man One snorted in the darkness.

"I was dead once."

"Dead?" said Man One fearfully.

"I'm sure I was. I went though deep water and was somewhere else, and I heard horses riding in the wind. The wind was death, I know it. There were horses in it. The horses of death. They came through the jungle and were all around me but they didn't trample me. I must have been a spirit or they would have trampled me. I'm sure I was a spirit. Dead."

"Not dead."

"Not now, but then I was. I was a spirit, a ghost, a man without a body."

"No."

"You don't believe in spirits? No, of course you don't. Communists don't believe in stuff like that. But it's true. I was a spirit. I was in the jungle."

Man One shivered. "There are spirits in the jungle," he said softly.

It was a perfect English sentence.

Charlie's heart jumped. Through all of his lessons, Man One had volunteered no information and said not a word in opinion; he had only repeated after him a phrase here, a word there, a complete sentence. This was their first real conversation.

"You too?" he said. "You feel them out there too, the spirits in the jungle?"

"There are spirits."

"Are you frightened out there at night?"

There was silence.

"You are, aren't you?"

"Uh-huh."

Man One had remembered his all-American word, then.

"You know what we always said? The night belongs to Charlie. We always said that. We thought you were the spirits."

Man One made a little negative noise.

"What are they then? What are the spirits?"

"The dead. They are the dead." It was a whisper.

Charlie felt a rush of pity for Man One. He spent every night of his life out in the jungle. He must spend his life afraid. He coaxed him to say more but Man One had fallen silent; he refused to speak of it further. Charlie could feel the fear inside him. He pitied him and loved him for his fear.

The day Man One came for his last lesson Charlie had known he was coming soon, sensed he was on his way, smelled him long before he heard his silent movements in the outer darkness. He had something very important to teach him that day and was excited about it. He had thought about it a long time and had the lesson plan organized in his head. He couldn't quite bring it to mind right now but he would, just as soon as he got himself down the access tunnel to the bars.

He made a great effort, but his bones were too

heavy to move so he left them behind and went down there with just his body on, very light and floating through the tunnel.

Man One was suddenly afraid. Charlie could hear his teeth shiver in his head and felt him slide away backwards, leaving only the smell of his terror behind.

Charlie was disappointed. He had badly wanted to talk to him today. He reached out his hand to Man One through the grid and his body went after it, flowing out around the bamboo bars like a mist, and followed him.

Man One was in a panic. He scuttled away ahead, making little fearful noises behind the gap in his teeth.

So Charlie stopped following and let himself float free; and he was very light and went upwards through the roof of the tunnel and through the packed dirt and he was not surprised by it, or afraid. He felt the dirt as he went through, layer by layer, and he had been right: his hole was very deep inside the earth. But after all it didn't matter. He had discovered how the fever had changed his body. It had loosened him on his bones. He was now so lightly attached that he could leave them behind and go up out of the earth.

It was so easy he laughed aloud at all the time he had spent down there not knowing.

He would go and find his son.

HOW HE SAW THE FLIGHT FROM DANANG

It was dark outside in the air, but with a darkness that was not dense and thick like his hole had been. This darkness had a diaphanous quality. It was smooth like silk and very fragile. He moved through it rapidly, propelled by some force he didn't comprehend. He seemed to be travelling on his back and he twisted as he went, looking down at the dark earth below.

It was a long way down and he watched for the signs of war, the flashes and the sudden flame, but there was nothing, just the rushing of his passage.

Fear flickered momentarily inside him. What if he got lost? What if he could never find his bones again? But what did he care for his bones? They were heavy and buried in the earth. He felt fit and vigorous and very light. He was overwhelmed by the exuberance of sudden freedom. He willed himself to travel faster, faster, faster than a speeding bullet, faster than the speed of light, out, out beyond the cosmos.

He shouted with joy. He was going to find his son.

The speed intensified and he braced himself

for the drag against the atmosphere, for his body to stretch out long and his eyelids to flatten and his lips to reverberate. But his hurtling body rushed against nothing. There was the knowledge of speed and the sound of rushing but not the sensation on his body.

At the point where he thought that his mind could encompass such speed no longer, there was a sharp crackling around him, like static on a radio. It grew louder and higher and he burst through something unseen with a flat booming sound, and stopped.

It was light on the other side with the soft shadowed light that comes before the dawn. Far off to the east he saw the sparkle of the sun's first rays on ocean. It was bright but he didn't need to turn his face away; his eyes could take it all in.

Beneath him was a denseness that he knew was land. But the land seemed to be moving and shifting and he was too high up to see what it was. He moved his arms experimentally and found he could maneuver his body sideways, then backwards and forwards. He found that if he raised his arms above his head he would slide down. He settled lower in the air.

There was a thick white mist lying low over the coastal water and the shifting of the land was the rushing of people. In a continuous packed horde they ran into the mist and vanished, like lemmings over a cliff.

He lifted his arms again and he was down

amongst them. No-one saw him. They ran at him with frightened, unseeing eyes and he felt the swish as they passed on through him. He knew that Minh was somewhere in that crowd with his son and he searched for her. But there were too many and he could not find her. The people ran and ran through him, with their mouths frightened and their hands spread out like twigs on branches.

There was a commotion in front of him: a dog barking violently with fangs bared and lips drawn back in terror. The crowd ran on around the animal. It was a common yellow-tailed cur, a slinking thieving creature and it stood there with its haunches set and the bristles standing up in a row down its back like the clipped mane of a horse, barking and barking.

Charlie realized then that the dog could see him. He spoke to it soothingly.

"It's okay, boy," he said. "There now, boy."

But the dog gave a high yip and laid its ears flat, backing off a couple of furtive steps. Charlie moved towards it and it turned tail and skittered off between the rushing legs.

Charlie, wanting to see what would become of it, stretched down his arms and pushed at the air. He surged upwards and hovered over the crowd, underneath the heavy blanket of mist.

The dog shot out of the crowd at the edge of the dock. With its legs still running, it fell down into the water below. It began to swim away from shore. Its eyes rolled in fear and it beat at the water, swimming and swimming against the heavy rolls and surges of the laden boats packing the harbor.

The crowd at the edge of the harbor noticed the dog and people began to shout to it, calling out encouragement to the dog who also wanted to escape from the enemy at their back, a wise dog.

Charlie swung out over the water, intending to come around in front of the creature and scare it back towards the shore. But a speedboat beat him to it. It swung in a big arc towards the dog. There was a man standing in the bow, pointing and shouting over his shoulder. He was white. He must be an American. Another man joined him, a big black man, a solid man. For a moment Charlie thought he was Harold T. Booker but then he saw he was too old, in his thirties maybe, ten years too old.

The two Americans called to the dog as they circled in on it and then the white one scooped it out of the water and dropped it into the bottom of the boat where it crouched, backing away from him and snarling.

The crowd on the shore let out a cheer and the white American waved. The boat swung away and headed out to sea, bouncing over the ocean. The big black man turned his head and watched the crowd on the shore until the boat was out of sight. His body was hunched forward and seemed to sag. Once he passed his hand over his eyes.

Watching him, Charlie understood that the Americans had abandoned Danang. The people were fleeing from the northern army.

And somewhere down there he could feel the presence of Minh and his son.

He swung back over the boats as they jostled about together, making the harbor a tiny place: tugs and sampans and fishing boats, barges and merchant ships with foreign names, navy ships and tiny improvised tubs and home-made rafts of corrugated iron nailed and roped to blocks of wood to make them buoyant. And they were all packed with bodies, shoving at each other and fighting to maintain position and keep intruders off, pushing them away as they paddled themselves up alongside, desperate men on inner tubes, and women flinging up their babies, hoping to find mercy for them amongst the lucky ones with a place on board.

Rafts, loaded beyond hope of balance with people and bicycles and motorbikes and baskets full of life's possessions, swamped and overturned. Many voices cried out and bodies fell off the edges of the higher boats like pennies thrown to dive for. Some struggled there a while and then relaxed and bobbed gently off, bumping up against the sides of other boats and barges, jostling up against the docks. Others just fell down and vanished under the slick grey water. And all the time more people crowded onto the docks and more people rushed onto the boats and more people fell down into the water, littering the bottom of the harbor with their bodies.

Charlie searched from boat to boat amongst packs of people grown vicious in their terror; people crying and shouting and killing each other for their chance to escape.

But Minh and his son were like wraiths, always somewhere just beyond the corner of his eye. He could hear them calling but he could not find them.

He searched the crowd on the shore, desperately flitting above the bodies, searching one agonized face after another until he knew he would not find her there.

Where then? He threw back his head and shouted Minh's name over the din.

No sound came from his throat but a sudden hush rolled over the crowd and a thousand faces turned upwards, looking fearfully through him at the sky.

There was a tremendous jerk between his shoulders as though some enormous hand had seized him. He rushed upward and the faces below grew suddenly tiny and then invisible.

He was running down a road. There was danger coming close behind and his heart pounded in panic. He ran with a crowd of others, surrounded by them, hedged in by the gasping of their lungs, the pounding of their feet, the smell of their sweat and fear. His body felt small and slight and his legs ached.

Something fluttered between his legs, slowing him down. He reached down with his right hand as he ran, clutched a handful of the torn white *ao dai* and held it up out of the way as he ran and ran down the road.

There were dead people on the road. The crowd stumbled and parted to flow around their bodies.

Once it was a child, once a soldier in a uniform, once a woman with the side of her head torn away.

He could hear shooting out beyond the crowd, single shots and the sound of automatic fire, from time to time a high wail, a shrill cry, and the continuous sound of babies screaming.

Once, off to the side of the road, the head and shoulders of a huge statue of the Buddha gleamed white over the heads of the rushing people, mocking them with the serenity of its gaze. Apart from that, he could see nothing beyond the great tumult of people around him, running with him, fleeing for life, clutching at bundles and the arms of small children. Don't let go of the children or they will be trampled to death.

He tightened his grip on the small arm he clutched in his left hand and ran and ran. The child stumbled and Charlie swept him back onto his feet without breaking his stride. He ran and ran down the road, running and running until he thought his heart would explode.

Again the giant hand seized him between the shoulders. He was jerked to a halt and then swept up and back from the running crowd. And it seemed to him that he came out of a slight girl in a torn white *ao dai* who ran and ran, with her hair flying up behind her. With one hand she held the *ao dai* away from her legs. With the other she dragged a small child behind her as she ran. It was a boy.

The crowd swallowed her up, running away from him, running and running down the road.

Charlie hovered above the road, watching the crowd run away from him. From up here he could see the reason for the sounds he had heard, the shots and screams. The road had heavy jungle on each side and the shots came out of the jungle. He could not see the guns or the shooters, just heard the sounds of firing and saw the flashes against the green undergrowth. And he saw the people on the edges of the crowd fall one by one, and the stragglers coming behind, the old and the weak and the very young.

The hidden shooters in the jungle picked off the crowd the way wolves pick off stampeding sheep. The smell of death was in the air.

Ahead of the crowd, Charlie saw the road stretching off into the distance, the silent jungle waiting all along the sides. And the crowd ran and ran away from him down the road, dying as they went, littering the road behind with the debris of the fallen. On and on they went, on and on. And they were small and gone.

There was a sharp clang and a tearing pain in his head and he was jammed back onto his bones with a force so great it knocked all the wind out of him.

"Danang has fallen. The people are running away from the city." Charlie blinked in the candlelight and watched Man One's face.

It was blank.

Man Two asked a question and Man One shrugged his shoulders, refusing to answer. But Man Two's voice was harsh, demanding that he speak.

Man One looked doubtfully at Charlie and then he told Man Two what he had said. Charlie knew he was telling it because he could hear the English words inside his head overlaying the Vietnamese like an echo as he spoke.

Man Two's head jerked back and he stared hard at Charlie. He said something to him in a shrill questioning voice. It was the first time he had spoken directly to him and Charlie felt suddenly afraid of him. He looked at Man One.

"He says, how you know this thing?" Man One said.

Charlie hesitated. "I saw it in a dream."

Man One spoke to Man Two again, making little back and forth movements with his hand.

Man Two snorted and tossed his head to one side. He spat on the ground. Charlie watched Man One but he could feel Man Two's eyes on him. He turned his head and looked directly at him. Man Two seemed to recoil and he flicked the end of his rifle.

Charlie wanted to cower back but he held his body so it didn't move. They watched each other tightly.

Then Man One laughed. He rocked on his heels, flapped a hand at Man Two and said some dismissive words. Man Two looked across at him and the tension broke.

Charlie felt a surge of affection for Man One. He was grateful to him. Man One was a good friend. He reached out and took him by the arm and Man One let him hold it a moment before he shook him off, awkward with embarrassment.

Had Danang fallen then? Or not? Was it a dream or his imagination? A fantasy brought on by illness? A fever in the brain? Had it fallen, though? Charlie lay in the dark obsessed with wanting to know.

When Man One came alone, he asked him.

"Has Danang fallen? Tell me."

And Man One answered him directly.

"No."

But how would he know? Charlie asked himself. He was just a jungle wraith, a hider in tunnels. How would he know about the progress of the war?

"Yes. Danang has fallen."

"No."

"Yes. I have seen it. It was not a dream. I saw it. I was there."

"No."

"You must make inquiries and tell me. Please."

"No." Man One's voice was frightened. "No."

HOW HE SAW THE FALL OF A GREAT CITY

He had seen Minh. And he had seen Danang. He knew the city. The Americans had abandoned it. The people were flooding south out of the highlands. He knew that it was so.

But Man One and Man Two did not believe it. Surely if it were true they would know. They were Viet Cong: surely they would know of such a major victory for their side?

Perhaps the news hadn't got to them yet. Yes, that must be it. But soon it would. News of a major victory like that would travel fast. It would come quickly out into the jungle and run through the networks of tunnels like a ferret after a rabbit. It would bring new heart to the fighters and make them fight harder.

Next time they came they would tell him. They would be proud of it and they would tell him. They would want him to know that they were the winners. They would gloat and tell him that he had been right after all. Because he was. He had seen the people. And Minh was with them. He knew it was her. He had found her. He had lost her again, but he had found her for a moment. Soon, perhaps, he would find her and not lose her. He would go with her and she would lead him to his son.

The child whose arm he had held had not been his son. He knew that too. His son was still a baby and that child had been five or six years old.

But he had felt his son's presence very strongly. Had someone else in the crowd been carrying him? Someone strong, perhaps a man who had taken pity on a girl running and carrying a baby in her arms? Had they traded children? Surely not. A father would cling to his own son when there was danger. A mother would too, even if it was hard to carry him.

Charlie puzzled over it but could make no sense out of it.

Five or six years old the child had been...five or six years...five years...or six years...years...five or six years...

His heart pounded. Had he been down here that long?

And then it dawned on him: he had seen the future. The child was indeed his son and he had grown the way children do. When danger came, Minh had taken him by the arm and run with him towards the south, one among so many. And he had seen it. Somehow he had seen it.

He told himself he should be amazed or afraid at this but it did not seem to him to be an amazing or a fearful thing to see the future. He did not understand it but there were many things he did not understand and he was not amazed or afraid of them either. He did not understand how television worked or how a dream could be inside a head and be as large as life. He did not understand calculus or the theory of relativity or the new theories of disorderly systems or trigonometry or black holes in the universe or any one of a million scientific things. He did not understand why people laughed sometimes or why they fell in love or got depressed or failed in their exams for no apparent reason or changed their minds without a second thought. He didn't even understand himself. He didn't understand how he had died and come alive again. And now he didn't understand how he had seen the future.

He had seen it.

He had seen the people and he had felt their fear as they ran down the road towards the south, looking for safety, dying as they went. He worried for them, remembering how they had fallen one by one to the bullets coming from the jungle.

Had Minh fallen? Or was she running still, dragging his son by the arm? Was the boy running alone now? Running and running down the road on weary little legs? Would someone help him or would he run and run until he fell behind the crowd and was picked off by the guns in the jungle and left there rotting on the road? Or would he be strong and run and run inside the crowd until they got to safety?

But safety where? Where were they going?

South. They were going south. They were going to Saigon.

And what would happen to Saigon? Would it fall too? Had it fallen already? Had his son died there, alone? Was the war completely lost?

He knew it was, had known it ever since he had been taken. But it had gone on until his son was five, maybe six. He marvelled. It had been a long war.

And what if his son had survived the road and the fall of Saigon too? What would happen to him now?

He remembered then how adamant Minh had become after the child was born. She would go to America with him.

"His name is Charlie," she had said. "An American name for an American boy."

Charlie remembered how she had left something unspoken and how he had felt that it was something important and how he had not asked. Then he remembered how her father had scorned the child as an American half-breed; how he had been ashamed of him and of his daughter too.

Then Charlie understood why Minh had been so determined to have her son grow up an American boy in America: her son would never belong in his own country.

And if the communists took the south, or if they had taken it already, the life of an American half-breed would be hard indeed. He would be only refuse left behind by the enemy, a constant reminder of the death and destruction of many years, a target for resentment and blame.

Charlie wanted urgently to help. How could he help?

His head ached, a still dull pain at the base of the skull. He lay there and imagined how his son would be tormented and scorned, how he would grow up full of anger and frustration, a man with no learning, no understanding, no civilization. He would become a fringe dweller, an outcast from society, an animal.

He berated himself for what he had done to his son and the pain in his head grew worse and worse. It became a band around his head, squeezing his temples tighter and tighter.

The top of his head clanged open and a hot wind whipped across it. Immediately he was catapulted into a furious, travelling darkness with a drumming underneath it, as if of rain. Great booming shapes swirled and erupted and rushed towards him and away. The atmosphere crackled with a harsh electric sound. Three times there was a shattering crash and a slash of brilliant light raced off into the distance with an angry spume of sheeted brilliance in pursuit.

He couldn't tell if it was the rush of his passage or the rush of the storm that ripped it up and away at such speed, but it was gone in the distance with a crack and a rumble and then there was silence.

He was over a big city and it was sunset. Soft rose and palest yellow faded gently into blue on the horizon. The air was cool and crisp. It smelled of cordite.

There was fear in the city and the war was here. It had come in from the countryside and was outside the city, coming in. He saw flames and smoke and rockets carving perfect arcs below him. A single plane above him arced the sky. The air was frantic with the sound of firing and a commotion of voices crying and calling to each other. "This way! This way!" they called. "They are coming from the north!"

And a great crowd of people ran through the city towards the south. But there they met people crying, "To the north! To the north! They are coming from the south!" And the crowd swirled and rushed and swept back towards the north.

A cry went up, "Lost! Oh, lost!" and he saw the people flee from the city and out onto the ocean.

And Charlie, watching, wept; and his tears became a roar and a great whirling wind came out of the sky and he was sucked into it and spun around and around. His ears were filled with a beating sound, as of many helicopters, and voices calling and calling and cursing him. And then it was silent and he went down and down.

He was on a beach. It was night now. A weak moon trickled miserably down the sky. Behind him the black-shadowed shapes of sandhills hid the horizon. The beach shone with a ghostly pallor and the water stretched out flat and black and still.

There were voices on the water, and lights, and something happening that he could not discern. There were shapes moving and sudden commands, a thump, the sound of a woman crying, suddenly silenced. Behind the sandhills a dog began to howl.

Charlie felt a prickle of fear and turned towards the sound but there was nothing, only the dog's voice climbing up towards the moon.

There was a splashing behind him and he turned back towards the water. Someone was running through the shallows, a woman. No, there were two people. Someone was chasing her, a man, spraying water up around him in flat shining sheets.

Charlie knew who the woman was before he saw the face. It was Minh, running in a panic back towards the beach. She was near the water's edge now and the pale moon shone on her face. A young boy ran with her, a lad of twelve or thirteen, half hidden by her body and the spray of water. His son?

The moon shone, too, on the face of the man behind them. It was Man Two.

Charlie gasped. Horror squeezed his lungs together. He cried out, "Minh!"

Man Two came out of the water behind Minh and the boy and watched them run. He was wearing a uniform and held his rifle in both hands. As they reached the dry sand and started off across it he raised the rifle, aimed and fired.

The shot made a high echoing sound and Charlie saw the bullet come out of the end of the rifle and travel slowly through the air behind Minh. He shouted to her again but she kept coming, with her arms stretched out and her face blank with fear.

When it hit her she was lifted off her feet. Her arms flung out from her body and her hair spread out like a peacock's tail. The horrified eyes were the same as the first time he had seen her flying towards him down the Danang street on a backdrop of flame. She fell onto the sand and skidded face-down to his feet, arms pushed back to her sides by the impact. Her hair, flung forward over her head, was a black stain on the gleaming sand.

The boy fell with her, rose, stumbled and, half-kneeling on the sand, turned up his face to Charlie. His face was the face of Man One.

Their eyes met and locked for a moment and it was the ancient child again, the same child who had taken him on the jungle path so long ago. Then he was up and running back towards the water.

Man Two watched him come, turned with him as he ran past into the water. He raised his rifle again and aimed at the boy's back.

Charlie lunged towards him but there was no-one there. He felt himself spinning again, going downwards, back into the earth.

His bones hurt and his body didn't fit properly. He was cold and hot and the sweat ran down into his eyes. He had found his son and he had lost him again. He did not know if he was dead or alive. He did not even know who he was any more or whether he had a son at all.

He lay there, flat and exhausted, and waited for Man One and Man Two to take him west to Hanoi.

"When will I go west?" he asked when they came next.

Man One looked quickly at Man Two. "When is safe," he said and made an upward sweeping movement with his hand towards the roof of the hole. He smiled at Charlie and his eyes were kind. Charlie yearned towards him.

Man Two spoke some quick hard words out of an angry face and Man One stopped smiling. He rolled open the bundle with the food.

Charlie turned his face away.

"Eat. You eat now." Man One's voice was as tender as a mother's.

He had brought a sort of rice soup, a watery gruel. The smell made Charlie's stomach heave.

"Good," said Man One and his voice was sad. "You eat." He set the bowl on the ground. "Sit," he said. "Good food." And he slipped an arm under Charlie's head, supporting him.

It was too much for Man Two. He lunged

forward and jerked Man One aside. Man One fell backwards against the side of the hole and Man Two snatched up the little bowl of soup. He waved it at Charlie and the soup slopped over the side of the bowl. His eyes were cold and hard and his words were harsh, directed first at Man One and then at Charlie.

Then he drank the soup himself and flung the bowl down on the ground. He belched, a long high sound that echoed around the hole, and the smell of it hit Charlie like a punch in the belly. He twisted over and began to retch.

Man One was back on his haunches and shouting at Man Two. Their argument went back and forth, loud and accusing, while Charlie threw up bile onto the ground.

Then they went away.

HOW HE WENT WEST TO HANOI

No-one came to his hole now. Charlie drank all the water in his canteen and lay on the floor, waiting. He willed himself to leave the hole and go once more in search of his son. But he was too weak.

He waited to die again. If his son was dead perhaps he would be able to find him then. If not, then he would look for Minh. But he would not come back again this time.

He had no more pain or itching and his bowels had dried up. He was beyond remorse and sorrow. He floated above his bones, swaying slightly like a balloon tethered to a post. His body seemed to have taken on a phosphorescent quality. A soft blue glow hung around him as he lay there staring into the dark like a man in a trance, watching, listening.

Strange images drifted in and out of his consciousness. Sometimes they were clear and separate, sometimes jumbled together, and sometimes they overlaid each other.

He thought he saw a man running through a forest, tripping and stumbling, turning his head fearfully over his shoulder.

He saw people laboring in a field, digging in hard ground with their naked hands. There were children there too, working with them.

He saw people weeping at an open grave. Their heads were shaven blue and they wore long grey robes. He could not tell if they were men or women. The sounds of their lamentation filled the air but he could not see into the grave or tell for whom they wept.

He saw children with American faces scrabbling in a ditch. They were collecting things, plastic bags and bottles running muck. There was the stench of sewage in the air.

He saw people in cells and cages, packed in so they could barely move. Some of them were sleeping or dead, propped upright by the crush of bodies. They were all Vietnamese people, people with smooth faces.

He had flashes of stubbled faces too. Some were white and some black and their cheekbones stood out like the winged roots of forest trees. They were Americans. He could hear them talking to him but he couldn't pick out the words. Their voices made a low continuous burring sound in the earth walls of his hole, like a gentle vibration, and sometimes he felt that they were with him there. He felt that he was being watched and sometimes hands moved on his body but when he reached to feel who touched him, no-one was there. He moved his hands out, grasping at the darkness, but they closed on emptiness.

Sometimes he thought he saw a shape or shapes beside him, misty in the blackness, but they dissolved as soon as he became aware of them. He never could turn his head fast enough to catch one in his vision.

One day he saw what could only have been a prison camp. It was large and sprawling with some big buildings and many small ones. The roofs were made of tiles. He could see the details of them very clearly.

There were people going in and out of the buildings and a lot more walking around what must have been an exercise yard. They were all men. Some of them were Vietnamese but many were American. He recognized some of their faces. He had seen them before in flashes. These were the men who talked to him in the walls of his hole. They were very thin.

They lined up in a row and went off through a gate away from the camp and he could not see where they went.

At first Charlie thought this must be the prison in Hanoi where he would go but no, there was water all around the camp. It was on an island. He puzzled over it. Such a big prison camp on an island. He had never heard of it.

He rolled out the map of Indochina behind his eyes and looked for the island but he couldn't remember. There was only the blue water stretching away from the land.

The water glinted under the sun and there were boats on it, people becalmed on an endless sea. A sudden urgency seized him. Somewhere down there in one of those boats was his son. He was sure of it.

As he watched, the sun fell down behind the ocean, leaving behind a broad stripe of red, and then it was gone. The sky dimmed and darkened and there were voices calling over the ocean, overlaying the murmur of American voices in his walls.

There were lights over the water too, soft and glowing and Charlie realized that he was with them. He had left his bones again without realizing. He looked down at his body, expecting the familiar glowing blue outline, but it wasn't there. Instead he was a golden color and not shaped like himself at all, just a ball of soft golden light like the lights around him.

He watched as they went in and out of the water, calling and calling, their voices like the twitter of many birds. And he understood that these were spirits looking for their bodies.

He went down into the ocean with them, down very deep until he came to the bottom and what he saw there made dread catch at his heart.

There were mountains under the ocean and the sides of the mountains were littered and strewn with the wreckage of many little boats. The dead lay all around, their bodies moving gently with the movement of the water and the long hair of the women streaming out to follow changing currents.

They lay with open expectant eyes as though watching for the return of their spirits.

Charlie began to search for his son. He went up and down the mountains examining every small figure. He searched for days and years, then many years, but he didn't find him. And at last, when the flesh had all dissolved off the waiting bodies and been eaten away by crabs and foraging bands of fish, he returned to the surface of the ocean.

The high searching song of the spirits was hushed now. The spirits wandered disconsolately, wailing softly over the haunted ocean, mourning for their lost bodies.

But Charlie was not ready yet to mourn. He raised his voice, calling to his son.

"Vuong," he called, using his son's Vietnamese name. "Vuong, oh Vuong, where are you, my son?"

"Chah-ree. Chah-ree." It was a loud voice and a strong hand was on his arm, shaking him.

He came back so suddenly that his whole body leaped upwards off the floor of his hole in a great twitching jerk and then fell backwards, trembling and uncoordinated. He struggled to control it.

"Chah-ree." It was a whisper now.

He turned to see and Man One was beside him, holding him by the arm the way he had held the arm of his son when he fled with him on the road from Danang.

"Come Chah-ree. We go now."

Man One had come alone. He had a candle and the look on his face was very strange.

"Come," he said again, pulling urgently at Charlie's arm.

Charlie began to cry. "My son is gone," he said. "I have searched and searched but he is gone. I have lost my son."

"Okay. Is okay," said Man One softly, patting his arm. "Not lost. Is okay."

Charlie felt Man One's hand on his arm, comforting him, and he loved him for it.

"What is your name?"

There was silence and Charlie held his breath. There was no answer, as there always was, but Charlie knew now. Man One had answered when he called. His name was Vuong. He was his son.

He examined Man One's face in the flickering light, admiring the planes of his face and the strength of its shadows, his ability to live like this and be a man. He was a son to make a father proud. Charlie smiled up at him, but Man One's eyes were black hollows in a hollow face.

"Come, Chah-ree."

Charlie didn't want to go. He wanted to stay

here in his hole where he was safe and warm and teach his son. It was his home.

"Must come now." Man One's voice was imperative.

Charlie smiled. Of course he would come. This man was his son who loved him. He would follow him anywhere. He pulled at his bones, struggling mightily with their weight.

Man One had a flask of water with him. He didn't pour it into the canteen as he usually did, but set it to Charlie's lips and poured it into him instead. And it seemed to do him good. His life came back and he made a great effort and picked up his bones.

Man One picked up his boots, tied the laces together, and strung them around his neck.

"Here. These you must need."

Charlie followed him down the tunnel from his hole, going west to Hanoi.

Man One went in front. They travelled slowly, in total darkness, and Charlie was not disoriented. It felt natural. He had become a mole, shunning the light.

They went in and out and up and down and Charlie followed Man One as easily as if he could see him. He took care not to push with his rotten toe but when he did, by accident, it didn't hurt.

Travelling was so easy that once he started to turn back, afraid that he had left his bones behind. He must go back and get them. But in turning he cracked his head sharply on the tunnel wall. He had his body with him then.

He crouched and crawled and let Man One pull him up through holes to higher levels and then down again to lower ones, and nothing hurt at all. He was euphoric, following his son.

He tried at first to remember how it had been when they brought him here. Were they now going up where they had gone down, down where they had gone up? He couldn't remember. The tunnels were as foreign to him as if he had never been through them. Each one was as narrow as the one before, so that his elbows scraped the walls, and just as low against his head. They zigzagged through them like a pair of sailing ships tacking against the wind.

Here and there they passed openings and from deep inside one of these Charlie thought he heard machinery, a heavy repetitious sound of metal against metal with a flat low swishing at the end. It seemed familiar somehow. A printing press? Down here?

On one stretch he was almost overwhelmed by the stench of human excrement. Several times he could have sworn the smell was blood. Once it was sweat. Once cooking. They met no-one though and heard no voices. There were no animals either. No bats or snakes, no ants, no centipedes, no rats.

No rats. He wondered about it. He had heard that there were always rats in the tunnels. His hole had been deep down and so that could have accounted for it, but they had come up several levels and he was sure that they were near the surface now. But still no rats. No, there were none. No rats. Where had they gone? He thought about the leg of chicken they had brought him. It had been a very small leg. And where would they have got chicken? Had he eaten rat? It hadn't tasted bad.

What about the other creatures? Come to think of it, there were no spiders either. The biggest spiders he had ever seen were in this country. He had seen them sitting in the trees like junior monsters, watching with their fat black eyes and holding their curved legs very delicately so that they barely touched the bark, the purple tip of one and then another drifting up from time to time as though they were so light that they might any minute float away; or jump down upon the neck of some poor unsuspecting soldier and throw him into apoplectic panic.

Did they eat spiders too? What would they taste like? Maybe not so bad.

Some of the shafts upwards and downwards to other levels had trapdoors over them and some didn't. He couldn't figure out what made the difference. The trapdoors he let Man One open for him. They were thick and heavy and bevelled on the edges so that they fit flush against the ground like a cork in a bottle.

They went on and on for what seemed to Charlie like

a very long time—hours—but maybe he was just confused. It couldn't have been hours. Most likely it had only been a few minutes. He couldn't tell at all. He just followed Man One faithfully until at last they stopped and Charlie sensed a solidness in front of him that meant the end of the tunnel.

He heard Man One's body shuffle ever so softly above him. He held his breath, listening to him go up. He heard the sound of a trapdoor lifted, soft as a spider's, and felt suddenly nervous. What if his son should leave him down here—as punishment for what he had done to him, abandoning him?

But no, Man One slid back down beside him.

"Go, Chah-ree," he whispered, his mouth so close to Charlie's face it was almost an embrace.

Charlie pulled back, afraid.

And then his son spoke to him in Vietnamese. *"Di di mau,"* he said.

Go quickly. How many times Charlie had shouted those words to cringing villagers, chasing them out of their homes. He was filled with dread. But his son's hand on his arm calmed him and he allowed himself to be pushed to the base of the shaft.

He turned there in the darkness.

"What is your name?"

And this time Charlie got his answer.

"Vuong." He barely heard the whisper.

"And your mother?"

A hesitation, then, "Mother is dead." He would

say no more.

It was enough though. Charlie turned away and, with Man One pushing from behind, made his way up the tall shaft and through the open trapdoor. He expected his son to follow, but instead he heard him reach up and pull the heavy trapdoor back down over his head.

Charlie panicked. He scrabbled around for the edge of the trapdoor but it was too well made. It fit flat on the floor of the tunnel as though it had never been there and he couldn't get a grip on the edge.

He did find wires though, fine and cunningly hidden. He grasped them in his hands, tensed to pull, and froze.

There was someone with him in the tunnel. He could feel him the way he used to feel Man One. He heard the heartbeat, the flicker of the eyelids, the held breath waiting to come out, the thoughts jumping in the brain. He smelled him too, the sweat and tension. He smelled his breath. He had been eating pork and beans: C-rations. He was an American.

Charlie was stunned. He crouched there in the dark with his knees around his ears and listened to his own kind, a man from another world.

Underneath him he could feel his son waiting. Why had he done this? Was he using him as bait?

And then he knew he wasn't. His son had let him go. He had found Americans in the tunnel and he had sent him up to them; he had sent him back home. Back home to Pauline.

He had to choose then, between Pauline and his son. But how to choose? He had forgotten how. He had been without choice for so long and so resigned himself to it that now it stared him in the face he was slow at it. Freedom to choose: a rusted function.

He found himself afraid, preferring not to have that freedom. He hesitated. Which one should it be? Pauline? His son? Which one?

In that frozen moment he heard the other backing out, slow and careful. It was time. Choose now!

Too late. He heard the pop of the pin and the roll of the grenade coming towards him. With a soldier's instinct he began to count.

One and breathe...and two and breathe...

He heard it come as clearly as if he had seen it. His sweat was cold on his temples and his heart was very still. His fists closed tight over the wires. He pulled the trapdoor up.

...and three and breathe...and four and breathe...

And slammed it down. Flung himself backwards away from it, twisting onto his face and curling up his legs as he went.

...and six and breathe...and breathe and breathe...

The world beneath him exploded. He heard the trapdoor fly out and smash against the roof of the tunnel, felt the blast, gasped to hold the air in his lungs as it was sucked away.

Something heavy fell on his head with a metallic crash. It was Man Two's magic bicycle.

HOW THEY TOOK HIM BACK

"We got a live one on the line here. Give a hand. Here he comes. We done got ourselves a living Charlie."

He was dragged out feet first, hands grasping at the blood-red dirt, torn reluctant from the earth's protective womb.

And lay there, spreadeagled at the tunnel entrance, arms sprawled wide and fingers curling upwards, head twisted back and down towards the darkness, blind.

He heard the chink of dog tags raised, released. He smelled the sharp sweet smell of soap. He felt his shirt pull open on his chest, dragged down by the neat bundle of Lou's letters, red across, green down.

"Well, I'll be damned! He's one of ours."

And then the crowding and the shouts.

"Will you just look at this?"

"God! What have they done to him?"

"Give him air!"

"Corpsman! Corpsman!"

"Call in a dustoff! Where's that radio?"

"Move it! Move it!"

And the gentle voices soldiers keep inside

them for their wounded.

"Hang in there, fella. You gonna be just fine."

"We got you back now, man. You gonna live."

"Easy there, go easy."

Strong arms of strong men holding him, lifting him, carrying him, carrying him away from his son, carrying him back home.

"You're doin' fine there, fella. Fine."

"Your war is over, you lucky motherfucker, you. You goin' home."

"Easy, easy now. Not far to go."

His rotten toe stuck up towards the light and all around he heard the weeping of the jungle.

Joanna C. Scott was born during an air raid over London, raised in Australia, and migrated to the United States in 1976 where she now lives and writes on a hill in semi-rural Maryland. She has a first-class honors degree from the University of Adelaide and a Masters in Philosophy from Duke University. She is the author of *Indochina's Refugees: Oral Histories from Laos, Cambodia and Vietnam*, and two novels, *Charlie and the Children* and *Pursuing Pauline*. She is at work on a third novel. Ms. Scott's poetry has appeared in such journals as *The Southern Poetry Review, The Ledge, California Quarterly, Poet Lore, Passager, Antipodes: A North American Journal of Australian Literature, Bogg: A Journal of North American and British Writing, The Baltimore Review,* and *The Lyric*. Her chapbook, *New Jerusalem*, was an award winner in Baltimore's Festival of Arts Literary Arts Competition. She has also won awards in the Chester H. Jones National Poetry Competition, the National Writer's Association Competition, the Passager Poet Competition and the Treasure House Dedicated Poet's Competition, and has been Director's Choice at the Westmoreland Arts and Heritage Festival Poetry Competition in Greensburgh, Pennsylvania. Steve Parish Publishing, Australia, features a selection of her poetry in a photographic calendar. Ms. Scott has three Australian children and three Korean, one large hairy dog, one small hairy dog, one tall cat, and one tolerant husband.